Death at the Rusty Nail

Veronica Vale Investigates - book 9

Kitty Kildare

K.E. O'Connor Books

Copyright © 2025 by Kitty Kildare

All rights reserved. No part of this publication may be reproduced, distributed, or transmitted in any form or by any means, including photocopying, recording, or other electronic or mechanical methods, without the prior written permission of the publisher, except as permitted by U.S. copyright law.

For permission requests, contact: kittykildare@kittykildare.com

The story, all names, characters, and incidents portrayed in this production are fictitious. No identification with actual persons (living or deceased), places, buildings, and products is intended or should be inferred.

ISBN: 978-1-915378-99-6

DEATH AT THE RUSTY NAIL

Chapter 1

"Your husband was a butcher?" I discreetly checked my notes to see if I'd recorded the deceased's occupation, but the information eluded me.

Benji, my ever-loyal dog, gave me a reproachful look, his head on his paws.

"A baker," my interviewee, Mrs Dawes, a tired-faced woman of thirty, said. "These are some of the last scones he made, God rest him. I kept them in the pantry, where it's cold. I wanted to save them for as long as I could. It's silly, I know. They're just scones, but they were one of the last things he baked."

"They're delicious," I said.

"How would you know? You've not had a bite of yours." Mrs Dawes pursed her lips. "And if you don't mind me saying, your mind isn't on this task."

"Why ever do you think that?" I shot a guilty glance at my neglected scone.

"You keep asking me the same questions. My Bernard was a plain man with simple pleasures. He loved his work and his family, and the occasional pint at the Blue Lion, when there was spare money, though we've not had much of that."

"I know the Blue Lion," I said. "It's close to one of my pubs."

"I thought you worked at the London Times. Isn't that why you're here?" Mrs Dawes asked.

"I have various occupations," I replied.

"I suppose lady journalism pays badly, if at all, so you must need another form of income."

Before I could answer, the parlour door sprang open, and three boys who looked as though they needed a good bath roared in, shouting and hollering. The noise assaulted my ears.

Benji jumped up, wagging his tail as the boys surrounded him.

"Is he safe to pat?" The lad asking was already ruffling Benji's fur.

"Out! Out! I told you I'm in an important meeting, and we're not to be disturbed," Mrs Dawes barked, brandishing a tea towel at the rampaging boys. "Play in the street until it's time for your tea. And no knockdown ginger. It upsets the neighbours."

"We're hungry!" one of them whined.

"Take my scone." Mrs Dawes handed it over without a second's hesitation.

"Have mine as well," I said. "If you don't object, Mrs Dawes. The scones look excellent, but I have little appetite."

One boy snatched the scone from my hand, tossed a piece to Benji, and they bundled out of the room, giggling together.

"I'm sorry about that." Mrs Dawes closed the door, which muffled the sound of the boys play-fighting as they headed outside. "Bernard was so good with them.

He'd take them out for hours on long walks to burn off their energy. Now it's just me, and I'm not sure what I'll do. I wanted a big family, but I always thought I'd have Bernard to help. It was a shock to all of us when he dropped dead while opening the bakery."

"He had just turned forty?" I checked my notes again. "You weren't aware he had a problem with his heart?"

"He complained of aches and pains, but we figured it was a sign he was getting old. The boys were a strain, too." Mrs Dawes dabbed at her eyes with a handkerchief. "Bernard left us provided for, though. This house is paid off, and we have the bakery. Although I don't expect I'll be able to run it on my own."

"It's remarkable what women can do when we put our minds to it," I said.

"Such as you working for the newspaper and running a pub, was it?"

"Something like that," I said. "Will you keep the bakery in the family? You could pass it on to one of your sons when they're old enough."

"Oh, I don't know. It may be easier to sell. Although the boys are in school, so I have some time. I'll think about it. It's always done a good trade. We have regulars, and they'll be sad if the place closes or changes hands."

"It's on the corner of Ashworth Street, isn't it?"

"That's right. Do you know it?" Mrs Dawes asked.

"No. But I'll stop by when you reopen and make some purchases. My mother enjoys her cake. So do I."

Mrs Dawes tilted her head. Although her eyes were red from crying, they had an intelligent gleam. "You said you had no appetite. Are you unwell?"

"No, I'm in good health," I said.

Her gaze ran over me. "I was going to say you could be in the family way, but most women get a glow about them, and you don't have that glow. You look tired."

"I'm busy. I've little time for afternoon naps and tea in the garden." The words snapped out of me, but Mrs Dawes didn't seem offended.

"I hear you there. But... I can sense something is wrong. I've not much of an education, but I've a way with people. Ever since we started this interview, you've been distracted."

"It's nothing to concern yourself with," I said. "I'll write an excellent obituary for your husband. He sounds like a solid chap and clearly has a family who adored him."

"I'm sure you'll do a good job. You came highly recommended. I asked friends and family who should write his obituary, and your name was mentioned several times. And Bernard always read the London Times, so I know he'd want to see his obituary in there."

"I appreciate the commendation," I said.

"You don't have to tell me if you've a mind not to," Mrs Dawes said. "But sharing a burden halves it. It's no good keeping everything close to your chest. I was always saying that to Bernard. He was a typical man and never talked about his troubles. I... I wondered if that's what caused his heart problems. Keeping everything inside was bad for him."

"An excess of emotion is just as bad as too little," I said.

Mrs Dawes settled her hands in her lap and regarded me steadily. I resisted the urge to tut. It was a technique I used when interviewing suspects and wanted them to open up. Most people grew uncomfortable with silence and would talk to prevent awkwardness. One often learned the most incredible things because someone wasn't comfortable with their own thoughts.

The sound of the boys playing in the street reached my ears. "How do you manage with so many children?"

"That was always my plan," Mrs Dawes said, not seeming surprised by the turn in conversation. "And I welcomed each of them. Bernard was an excellent husband, and he adored the boys."

"But how do you keep it all together?" I asked. "Even having one child must be a strain."

"Is that what's on your mind?" Mrs Dawes asked. "You're uncertain if motherhood is for you?"

"I've no interest in that, but I have a friend who is in the family way, and she's extremely unwell," I said. "I can't stop thinking about her and wondering if she made a dreadful mistake. If carrying the child is making her feel this poorly, how will she manage when there's an infant to care for?"

"Ah! That's your worry. Not all women have a comfortable pregnancy," Mrs Dawes said. "My last boy almost put me in the grave. I spent months on bed rest. It was dreadful. I like to keep busy, but the doctor said if I got back on my feet before the baby arrived, we'd both perish. That was when we called it a day and shut up shop, so to speak."

"A sensible choice." Now that I'd opened up, I couldn't stop. "My friend is suffering terribly, and the doctor is worried she may not be strong enough. What if, when the child is born, she grows even sicker?"

"Do I look sick to you?" Mrs Dawes asked. "I could barely lift a hand towards the end of my last pregnancy.

I'd get heart palpitations, sickness, and feel dizzy. As soon as my boy was born, it went away. That's what happens when you become a mother. The problems and struggles you go through no longer matter. You have this perfect, tiny person you're responsible for, and they depend on you. And you feel this love you've never felt before. It's a miracle."

"People have told me that," I said. "There must be an evolutionary mechanism that ensures a mother will continue to have children despite the birth almost killing her."

"Gracious. I don't know anything about that," Mrs Dawes said. "It sounds as though your friend is being looked after and has a doctor keeping an eye on things. I'm assuming she's on bed rest?"

"Almost. And although she complains about it bitterly, she's getting the best care."

"And the baby?" Mrs Dawes asked.

"Thriving. Growing fatter by the day if my friend's stomach is anything to go by."

"When she has the baby in her arms, it will all be worth it," Mrs Dawes said. "And if she's young, she'll spring back into shape. If not, there are always corsets."

"Perish the thought," I said. "Now, I've taken up enough of your time talking about my problems. I'm being selfish. You've just had a bereavement."

Mrs Dawes leant over and clasped my hand. "My dear, it's never a problem to help another. We don't know each other, but I saw you were struggling. I hope talking things through has comforted you, no matter how small."

Her show of warmth caused my eyes to mist, and I focussed on my notes until the tears vanished. "You're very kind."

"I'll freshen the teapot while you organise yourself. And I've some Battenberg cake in the pantry, if your appetite has returned."

Fifteen minutes later, I was composed, had completed the interview, eaten two slices of Battenberg cake, had a cup of tea, and was saying goodbye to Mrs Dawes. Her excessively noisy boys lurched outside the house, their thoughts most likely on food once more.

I headed away from the small but smartly turned-out terraced house with Benji. I'd parked a few streets from the dwelling to get some exercise before meeting Mrs Dawes.

Rather than heading to the car, Benji shot off in the opposite direction.

He was such a well-behaved dog, so I took his diversion seriously and followed. It became apparent he'd picked up on some plaintive mews. Kittens!

As Benji searched, I followed, my gaze darting from side to side. Benji turned right into an alleyway and nosed along the ground. A moment later, he stopped before a closed cardboard box with a brick on top.

I hurried to join him, crouching and giving him a well-deserved scratch behind the ears and a biscuit from my pocket. I flipped open the box lid and discovered four tiny kittens, their eyes only just open. Their mother hadn't left them here. Someone had abandoned them in this shadowy alleyway. Left to die.

My fury rose. I checked each kitten. They all appeared healthy, but were cold and hungry.

"The despicable nature of some people never fails to astound and disgust me," I muttered to Benji as I opened my coat and tucked the kittens inside to get them warm.

Benji whined softly and gently nudged the kittens with his nose.

"If I ever find the person who did this, they'll get more than a tongue-lashing." I buttoned my coat, ensuring the kittens were comfortable, then marched smartly along the alleyway and dashed to my car. I was glad the late afternoon wasn't too cold, or the kittens would already be dead.

Once inside, I kept them nestled against my chest and, with little regard for speed or other vehicles, sped through the London streets, back home. It wouldn't be the first time we'd picked up waifs and strays, so we were equipped to deal with such matters.

I parked and dashed inside, clutching the kittens close. From the damp warmth against my chest, one of them had had an accident out of fear or shock. It was of no matter. It would wash out. The most important thing was to save these kittens.

"Veronica, is that you?" my mother, Edith Vale, called from her downstairs bedroom at the front of the house.

"I'll join you shortly," I called back. "Where's Matthew? I have four kittens in need of his attention."

"Kittens? You said no more foster kittens!"

"I found them in an alleyway. I couldn't abandon them." I was already in the kitchen, hunting through the cupboards to find bottles, formula, and warm blankets. "Matthew, where are you?"

"I'm coming! I was busy upstairs." Matthew thundered down the stairs and jogged into the kitchen. His hair was in its usual messy state, suggesting he'd been raking his fingers through it. He wore a misbuttoned pyjama jacket, though he had suit trousers on underneath. His feet were bare. "What have you got there?"

"What does it look like? Help me! They need warming and feeding." I passed him two of the kittens and a clean blanket. We spent ten minutes focussed on ensuring those tiny, innocent creatures survived.

"You smell terrible," Matthew murmured, his gaze on a small black-and-white kitten that was suckling up the last of the milk he'd made for it.

"I'll change presently. The kittens don't seem to mind my smell."

"I do." Matthew wrinkled his nose.

"You can't talk. You wore that pyjama jacket yesterday."

"I've no one I need to impress," Matthew said. "Although you do. There are messages beside the telephone for you."

"Oh! Is it Lady M? How's Ruby?" I tensed, my gaze flicking to the hallway. "She hasn't taken a turn for the worse, has she?"

"One is from Lady M and another from Ruby herself. Ruby asked you to take her some perfume, and she wants half a dozen chocolate eclairs. She said the baby is demanding them."

I'd revealed to my mother and Matthew, on pain of death that they didn't gossip about it, that Ruby was pregnant and in hiding at Lady M's grand estate.

"She won't keep them down. She can barely manage plain broth," I said. "But I'll take them, just in case."

"And there are several messages from Maudie Creer."

"Our landlady at the Rusty Nail?" I asked.

Matthew nodded. "She said it's urgent she speaks to you."

I sighed as I gently rubbed a kitten to ensure it was warm enough. "Maudie can wait. She wants to start a book club at the pub. I told her there wasn't much call for it around those parts, but she's most insistent."

"Maudie didn't mention a book club," Matthew said. "She said it was urgent, though."

"One woman's urgency is another woman's flimflam," I said. "My focus is the kittens. And then I must visit Ruby. Maudie and her book club will be dealt with another day."

Chapter 2

I stared at the luxurious environs Ruby had sequestered herself in. In fact, I'd been staring at Lady M's mansion for ten minutes. I wasn't dallying because I didn't want to see Ruby, but things hadn't been the same since she'd hidden her pregnancy from me.

I'd done my best to keep a grip on my frustrations since Ruby was in a most delicate condition, but every time I spent more than a few minutes with her, my anger rose, and my tongue sharpened.

What was that irritating saying? You were always the unkindest to the people you were closest to? It had never made sense to me, but suddenly, it was as clear as day. Ruby had hurt my feelings. I shouldn't care about such a thing, with her health in such a precarious position. But since Lady M had summoned me after Ruby's health took a turn for the worse, I'd not been issued so much as an apology.

My fingers flexed around the steering wheel. "After this, Benji, we'll go for a long, bracing walk until we're too tired to think straight. That's what we need. Fresh air and plenty of exercise. All these ruminating thoughts do no good."

Decision made, I collected my handbag and climbed out of the car, Benji coming with me. He dashed ahead, always excited to see Ruby. I loitered behind, pretending to admire the flowers.

From inside the mansion came a delighted cry. It was Ruby, and Benji had discovered her.

A few seconds later, Lady M's butler appeared in the open doorway. He nodded politely. "Miss Vale. May I take your coat and handbag, or do you wish to remain outside for the duration of your visit?"

"I'll keep hold of them. I won't stay long," I said in a clipped tone.

He stepped back, giving me full access to the mansion. Lady M's wealth was substantial and came from many generations of landed gentry. Her husband had added to that fortune but had died years ago, and Lady M now reigned supreme over this vast estate, which covered more than one hundred acres. She rarely talked about her wealth, since she considered it vulgar, but I always found that the richest talked about it the least, so I could only imagine how much was in her coffers. Certainly enough to take in a pregnant, unmarried assistant without so much as an eyelid bat.

I braced myself, pulled back my shoulders, and ensured I was smiling before entering the blue parlour, in which Ruby had taken up residence during her confinement.

The room was stunning, with the walls painted in pale cream with blue wainscoting. Two large sash windows face the gardens, fitted with blue and cream striped silk curtains. The room contained a velvet Chesterfield sofa, a chaise longue, two cream wingback chairs, and a mahogany writing desk.

Ruby reclined on the chaise longue, her feet bare, her stomach swollen. Despite wearing makeup, she had the pallor of someone who had recently been dug up.

"There you are," she said too brightly. "I thought Benji had driven himself here."

"I was taking the air," I said. "You look... better."

"I look ghastly!" Ruby said this during every visit. "No matter how much powder and colour I add to my face, I look like one of those old maids in a pantomime. I refused to look at myself in the mirror this morning. It was all too shocking."

I perched on the edge of a chair opposite Ruby, gently waving away the butler's discreet enquiry as to whether I needed refreshments. "Is there any news from the doctor?"

"He's due any moment," Ruby said. "He'll say the same thing he did last week. Everything's coming along nicely. I need plenty of rest and nourishment, and the joyous day will be here before we know it." She sighed and played with a button on the voluminous dress she'd had tailored to mask her large bump.

"Then you have nothing to worry about," I said.

"I don't know what's wrong with me." Ruby glanced at me but didn't hold my gaze for more than a second.

"I'm sorry to say I have little experience in such matters," I said. "From what I understand, not all women find this situation as pleasant as they should."

"I'm wondering..." Ruby paused. "This isn't an ideal situation for anyone, but perhaps I'm being punished."

"By whom and for what?" I arched an eyebrow.

"Veronica! There's no need to be coy about this situation," Ruby said. "We're aware times are changing and women have more freedom, but I have no ring on my finger and no man to support me. Lady M pays me a reasonable wage, but to manage this situation alone is unsettling. Tongues have been wagging, and they'll continue to wag as my predicament evolves."

"I'm acutely aware of that, but I'm still unsure as to who is punishing you," I said.

"I've been reading from Lady M's extensive library. Perhaps it's the Fates or Karma. Maybe God or an archaic divinity who has stepped in to ensure I pay penance."

"For finding yourself in a situation that millions of women go through? What nonsense." I found religion to be of little comfort in trying times. Life had dealt some unkind blows, hardening my heart to the possibility of divine intervention. I recognised many people found comfort in such beliefs, but I was left questioning and unsettled rather than comforted. It would appear Ruby was in the same state. "This isn't a question you'll ever resolve, so why pursue it?"

"I must keep myself occupied," Ruby said. "Otherwise, all I do is lounge around and eat the delicious food Lady M supplies for me, and that'll do my waistline no good."

"It's doing the baby good," I said.

"If I keep anything down," Ruby said.

When I'd dashed home from my adventures in Kent, I'd discovered Ruby a sickly shadow. Any food made her violently nauseous, and she suffered dreadful headaches. Fortunately, with the careful ministrations of several doctors, she'd improved, though still suffered daily.

"You have a craving for chocolate eclairs?" I asked.

Her nose wrinkled. "I've rather gone off that idea. All the cream will curdle in my stomach."

I frowned, considering the box I'd left in the car. "It's of no matter. The bakery was out of eclairs when I stopped by."

"That's good. I don't want you to go to any trouble on my account."

"It wasn't any trouble," I said. "Isn't that what friends are for? We support each other."

"Absolutely. And I'm grateful for your support. Although I wish you'd visit more often. This estate isn't that far from your home."

"Life keeps me excessively busy," I said.

"You only came once last week! And you promised you'd visit at the weekend, but you never arrived. I sat by the window for hours, looking for your car."

I pressed my lips together. I'd sat in my car for half an hour, considering making the journey to Lady M's estate, but I had no enthusiasm to visit Ruby.

I'd been told on more than one occasion that I could hold a grudge, and it would appear I had a hefty one against my best friend. It made this situation most uncomfortable.

"Well, it's no matter," Ruby said breezily. "You're here now. Tell me about your adventures. Are you working on any exciting cases with Jacob?"

"He's working on an interesting fraud case, but he has everything in hand. We speak most evenings on the telephone, and he updates me."

"You must miss him, since he's so far away," Ruby said.

"He visits me, and I go to Kent on the train every other weekend. That's why I haven't been able to attend to you so often. And it's not as if you need me here, is it? You have Lady M at your beck and call, and all of her staff."

"It's not the same," Ruby said. "Lady M is my employer, and the staff are paid to do what they're told. That's not friendship. Not like we have."

I looked away. This friendship felt in tatters, and I had no idea how to repair it. Maybe there was no repair. Ruby and I were diverging in different directions. She was about to become a mother, and I'd carry on with my work, my private investigations, volunteering at the dogs' home, and helping my family. Ruby could no longer be a part of that now she had a new focus.

"What about cases you're looking into?" Ruby asked. "It's been a while since you've enjoyed a jolly good murder."

I slid her a glare. "Murder is never to be enjoyed."

"Oh, come now, what nonsense," Ruby said. "You're never happier than when you're chasing down a villain. The same goes for me."

"Well, you need to make adjustments," I said. "There'll be no chasing anyone once you're a mother. Well, you'll be chasing your infant once it walks, I suppose."

"Things won't change that much," Ruby said. "I'll still assist you."

I said nothing.

Ruby let out a sad little sigh. "That is, if you want me to."

A knock on the parlour door interrupted our conversation, and the butler showed Doctor Finnegan into the room. He was a short man, round with a bald head, with glasses and a receding chin. He was one of the best in the business when looking after ladies in fragile situations, such as Ruby's.

Doctor Finnegan nodded a greeting to both of us. "And how are we today, Miss Smythe?"

"Much the same, doctor," Ruby replied.

"I should leave," I said.

"Don't," Ruby said. "There are no secrets between us."

My breath felt sharp as I inhaled and rose from my seat. "I'll wait outside."

I didn't look back as I left the parlour since I didn't want to see Ruby's hurt expression. I'd seen it a lot recently, and it was because of my behaviour. But every time we met, I felt out of control. I was usually so adept at keeping my emotions stable.

I lingered in the garden with Benji for half an hour and was considering leaving when Doctor Finnegan emerged from the mansion. He pushed his glasses up his nose and strode towards his car.

"Excuse me, doctor. May I enquire how your patient is faring?" I hurried towards him.

He turned, his expression one of calm composure. "I have advised continued rest. Miss Smythe is eating again and drinking plenty of fluids, which is excellent. Although she mentioned being under-stimulated. Perhaps she'd welcome more visits from those close to her."

Ruby had been complaining about me to the doctor! "I thought it best not to overtax her. She gets excited easily."

"I am concerned about her nerves," Doctor Finnegan said. "Miss Smythe is unsettled. Either she's unaware of what vexes her, or she is unwilling to speak to me about it."

I looked down. I was supposed to help Ruby during difficult times. Instead, I'd made matters worse.

"Is there anything more you can do for her?" I asked. "A tonic? Or a stay in a hospital? Perhaps the sea air would do her good."

"I have considered all possibilities." Doctor Finnegan placed his bag in the car. "Believe me, I am doing the very best I can. The most important thing now is that she finds a way to settle those nerves. After the baby arrives, the illness will go away."

"Or become worse," I said. "As I understand it, motherhood is a trying time."

"Or a delight," Doctor Finnegan said. "It's a blessing. One all women should welcome, no matter the trials. Now, if you'll excuse me, I have another patient to visit."

I watched him start the car and drive away. Irritating man. He didn't truly know what a woman went through when she was with child.

"Excuse me, Miss Vale," Lady M's butler called from the open front door. "There's an urgent telephone call for you."

"Oh? How did they find me here?" I hurried into the house to pick up the telephone, which stood in the foyer. It must be my mother or Matthew.

"Miss Vale, I'm sorry for chasing after you."

It was Maudie from the Rusty Nail!

"Goodness. Is everything all right? You don't sound yourself," I said. "Now, before you complain, I received your messages. I intended to contact you. I'm assuming this is about the book club?"

Maudie sniffed loudly. "I have a problem guest, and she's causing me all manner of trouble. I've asked her to leave, but she's refusing. I don't like to burden you, but I need help."

"Have you telephoned the police?" I asked.

"They said it's not something they can deal with. Besides, I don't want them involved. They only poke and prod about in matters that don't concern them," Maudie said. "But I'm ever so worried about this guest. She's damaging the pub's reputation."

I glanced towards the parlour. I was of no help to Ruby at the moment. "Very well. I'll be right there." I ended the telephone call and collected Benji, who had returned to Ruby's side and was enjoying a belly rub. "We must go. I have a tricky customer to deal with at the Rusty Nail."

Ruby's expression fell. "That's such a beautiful building. We haven't been there in an age. You're leaving now? I wish I could help, but I'm worse than useless in this situation."

"You stay where you are. I'll be back as soon as I can."

My goodbye was stiff and cool. As I drove away, an ache of tension throbbed behind my eyes.

I always said I disliked change. It was painful and usually unnecessary, but this friendship had changed, and I feared it was broken and beyond repair.

Chapter 3

"This will put hair on your chest." Maudie Creer set down a plate of food and a glass of gin fizz on the rustic round table tucked in the corner of the Rusty Nail. We were near a small fireplace, with a faded picture of the River Thames hanging over the mantel.

Maudie was a no-nonsense woman who had worked at the Rusty Nail for almost twenty years. She started in the kitchen, but her aptitude with customers quickly earned her a promotion.

During the Great War, the pub's landlord was called up to serve and never returned. In his absence, Maudie took over and had remained in the role of landlady ever since. Since she'd taken control, profits had soared.

"Thank you. But I'm not here to dine." Although my gaze lingered on the large plate of pie and mash and the tempting gin fizz. I hadn't realised how hungry I was until she'd presented me with such delicious fare.

"You look worn out. Eat, and then we can talk." Maudie settled into the seat opposite with her plate of dinner and a pint of bitter. She also had a plate of scraps for Benji, which she placed on the floor, and he set to with delight.

"Is your problem customer currently in the bar?" I poked a knife into the top of my pie to allow the steam to escape.

"She's at the back, although you'll have a job seeing her." Maudie lowered her voice. "She's surrounded by gentlemen. Well, I use that term loosely. Some of them appear to be gentlemen, but their manners, once they've had a few drinks, leave a lot to be desired."

I peered through the crowd of evening punters. A peal of laughter caught my attention, and I glimpsed a woman of perhaps fifty. Impeccably groomed, she sported silver-streaked auburn hair and an elegant but understated ensemble.

"Is that the lady?" I nodded towards the woman.

"That's her. Cora Bellamy," Maudie said, frowning.

I took a sip of my gin fizz and tucked into my buttered mashed potatoes. "Is it the company she brings into the pub you don't approve of?"

Maudie finished her mouthful of food. "When I took her booking, Cora claimed to be a genteel woman who needed a restful break, but needed to be central, which is why she chose the Rusty Nail. She paid in advance, and it seemed aboveboard."

"How long has she been staying?" I asked.

"A few days." Maudie glanced over at Cora. "She's ever so unsettling."

"What is it about her behaviour that troubles you? If she's bringing in extra customers, it can only be good for our bottom line."

Maudie shuffled in her seat. "I have my regulars, and they hate the disturbance. Cora takes over, and she stays up late. On two occasions, she's asked me for a lock-in."

"I hope you didn't agree." I wouldn't object too violently if Maudie had an arrangement with Cora. Landlords often brought in a tidy sum hosting exclusive parties late into the night, provided the police didn't catch them.

"I agreed to the first one. I know I shouldn't," Maudie said. "But it was so rowdy, and Cora brought in lady friends. They weren't reputable. I poked my head into the room she'd hired, and I still can't get the images out of my head. It was shocking."

"What were they doing?" I asked.

"I can't say to a lady of your standing," Maudie said.

"I've seen a fair few frightful sights in my time," I replied.

"Bawdy business. I want her gone. I've asked her nicely to leave, but she said she plans to extend her stay. Things need to go back to normal. Too much upheaval is bad for everybody."

"I can't disagree with that. Have you offered her money back on the room?"

"Yes, but she refused to take it. She has plans that can't be changed. I was polite, then I was stern, and then I was rude, but she's not for budging. I got so het up the last time we had a confrontation, I didn't know what to do. That's when I telephoned you. I'm sorry for bothering you. I can usually handle tricky customers, but Cora has got the better of me."

"I'll finish my meal and speak to her," I said. "We have every right to ask her to leave if she's disrupting business."

DEATH AT THE RUSTY NAIL 23

"Thank you. And sorry again for the trouble." Maudie's gaze cut to the door, and she frowned. "There's one of her lady friends. She pops in most evenings."

I glanced over my shoulder and saw a striking woman in a fitted dress. Her face was heavily made-up, and her hair cascaded in glossy ringlets around a face that, on first glance, was pretty. But as I studied her, I realised the makeup concealed tiredness and wrinkles.

"Was she one of the friends at the lock-in?" I asked.

"Yes, and she was sitting on a gentleman's lap when I saw her," Maudie said.

We watched as the lady joined Cora and her gentleman friends. There was some teasing and more laughter before the woman received a drink and eagerly pressed a kiss to a man's cheek.

"I'll be back in a mo." Maudie stood. "Father Kersey's just shown up. He'll want his half of ale before evening mass. Some of these priests can be stuffy, but he does good work with the troubled communities in this part of London, so I make sure to do right by him."

Maudie hurried off to greet a tall, thin gentleman of around thirty with dark, receding hair. She served him his half-pint and then saw to several other customers.

"Good gracious! Is that Veronica Vale I see before me?"

I turned in my seat, and for a moment, I couldn't place the smartly dressed blonde woman standing there with a bemused smile on her face.

"Oh, for goodness' sake. Don't say you've forgotten me. The last time we met, we clashed over who was to interview that dreadful viscount with the stutter and the limp."

I stood, a smile crossing my face. "Camille Hartley! What brings you to my pub?" I held out my hand, and Camille took it warmly.

"Your pub? Oh, that's right. Your family is in the business. I'd quite forgotten." Camille glanced around. "I didn't realise you owned the Rusty Nail. I often come in here on my way home. Although I'm here on a matter of business this evening."

"My father bought this pub years ago. I'm running things now." I gestured for her to take the seat Maudie had vacated, and she joined me at the table.

"You're no longer writing?" Camille set down a smart brown handbag, the handle fraying at one seam.

"I'm still at the London Times writing the obituaries," I said. "I get a few extra pieces now and again. I manage that alongside the pubs."

"I suppose when you have a landlady as capable as Maudie, there's little you need to do," Camille said.

"Maudie is excellent," I said. "An asset to the business."

"It goes to show women perform as well as men. Sometimes better." Camille winked at me. "I've been pushing for a promotion at the Evening Standard. My boss keeps muttering about pay freezes and no roles for women. I've told him I'll leave. Go freelance if I have to. I know my value."

"It's a balancing act to show our worth and not put too many noses out of joint," I said.

"As if that would ever concern you!" Camille chuckled. "I understand there must be jobs for the men who came back from the war, but that shouldn't mean we're put out on our ear. It's unfair. We held everything together, and we shouldn't be slung out just because we've served our purpose."

"I couldn't agree more," I said. "It's much the same at the London Times."

"You have your uncle watching your back, you lucky old thing."

"He does what he can, but there's no favouritism," I said. "Well, a small amount, but he ensures there's a good amount of work for everybody. You said you're here for business?"

Camille leant forward, her eyes gleaming. "I have a few extra questions to ask one of your guests. I'm doing a piece on fashion history, and Miss Cora Bellamy is one of my interviewees."

"I didn't realise she was involved in the world of fashion," I said.

"Of her own making," Camille replied. "Cora is a self-taught seamstress. She makes all her dresses and has well-known ladies who buy from her. I wanted some local colour in the piece, so it wasn't all about the fashion houses and shows. Everyone talks about those, but I plan to show we have talent in this very district."

"What is your opinion of Cora?" I asked. "Did she cause you concerns when you interviewed her?"

"I can't say she did," Camille said. "She was pleasant. She offered me several drinks, and we had an agreeable few hours together. I wrote my outline, but I wanted to add more detail. Cora said I could visit this evening, but I see she already has companions."

"Yes, and that's a concern to Maudie," I said. "It's unsettling our regulars."

"The grumpy old buggers in this place don't like it when their favourite seats are taken. That's all it'll be," Camille said. "They still think I'm not local, and I've been coming here for years."

"Perhaps." My attention had returned to Cora. Just how far had her bawdy behaviour gone? Drink addles the senses, but she wouldn't do anything to ruin her reputation, would she?

"Well, I need to go." Camille stood and collected her handbag. "I'm meeting Cora in five minutes. It was good to see you. We should catch up properly."

"I'd like that."

We said our goodbyes, and Camille hurried away.

Maudie returned with fresh drinks and settled back into her seat. "Was that a friend of yours?"

"A fellow journalist," I said. "She's been interviewing Cora. I asked if she had concerns about her, but she picked up on nothing. Camille's a clever type, so she'd know if there were problems."

"I may not have the smarts, but I know people," Maudie said. "And I don't like that Cora one bit. I want her gone."

"Then we'll make it happen," I said. "I don't want you unsettled, not in your place of work. You look after everything so expertly."

"That's good of you to say. I can't think of anywhere else I'd want to work."

"Let's finish up and make a plan of action," I said.

We were ending our meal when a smartly dressed chauffeur, cap in hand, entered the pub. He went to the bar first, and the barmaid directed him to our table.

Maudie sighed. "Not him again. It's the third time this week."

"Who is that?" I asked.

"Lady Eugenia Fairfax's chauffeur."

"You don't like the man?"

"He's pleasant enough, but he's wasting his time." Maudie stood and thumped her hands on her hips. "Johnny, before you even ask, I haven't seen him. Try elsewhere."

The chauffeur, Johnny, stopped by the table, an apologetic look on his face. "Her ladyship insists I visit his favourite places and people, so here I am."

"Who are you looking for?" I asked.

Johnny's expression was curious as he took me in. "And you are?"

"This is Veronica Vale," Maudie said. "She's my employer, so watch your manners."

"Sorry, but this is a delicate situation," Johnny said. "Her ladyship will have my hide if she thinks I'm gossiping."

"You coming in here several times a week asking about her son isn't discreet," Maudie said. "Take my word for it. I haven't seen Tarquin."

"I have to check," Johnny said. "Her ladyship is in the car, and she's unhappy. Tarquin hasn't been seen for some time, and she's worried about him."

"This won't be the first time he's been a ninny," Maudie said. "He goes off on these larks with his chums, and when they run out of money, they come back with their tails between their legs."

"Tarquin Fairfax is missing?" I asked.

"No, he's not missing," Johnny said. "But Lady Eugenia has him on a tight lead. She doesn't like him spreading his wings. He's an adult, so he can make his own decisions. Unfortunately, those decisions aren't sensible, which is why her ladyship keeps such a close eye on him."

"Why do you think he'd be here?" I asked.

Johnny glanced at the table where Cora Bellamy held court.

"Oh, I see," I said. "He's acquainted with Miss Bellamy?"

"Not here, they're not," Maudie said. "I haven't seen the young man since Cora arrived. If someone of Tarquin's standing came to drink here, I'd know, and I'd charge him a premium, since he can afford it."

Johnny's smile was wry. "I'm sorry if I'm disturbing your evening. I don't suppose I could grab a quick half? I need something to wet the whistle. This is our first stop of the evening, and I fear it'll be a long one."

Maudie sighed but didn't complain as she led Johnny to the bar to fix him a drink.

I remained in my seat, my gaze intent on Cora, who was more visible since she'd made space for Camille and shooed away a couple of the chaps.

Cora Bellamy may have presented herself as a genteel woman seeking a rest, but this lady was keeping secrets and causing trouble at my inconvenience.

That must stop.

Chapter 4

"Miss Bellamy. May I have a word?" Despite marching to the table and making it clear I wished to speak to Cora, the men surrounding her and the lady in question remained obstinately oblivious to my presence.

Cora paused, her glass of champagne poised mid-air as her gaze finally shifted to me. "I don't believe we're acquainted." Her voice was rich and husky, with an undertone of humour.

"Indeed, we are not," I said. "I own the Rusty Nail. You'll see the family name on the licence above the door. I'm Veronica Vale."

"Well, isn't that something?" Cora took a sip of her champagne and placed the glass delicately on the table. "I enjoy meeting an independent woman. May I ask how you acquired the funds to secure such premises?"

Her boldness surprised me. "Perhaps we can discuss that another time."

"I thought you were one of the girls," a dark-haired, drunken man slurred. "Although you're too old for my taste."

"Manners!" Cora swatted him lightly on the back of his hand. "You must not speak to a lady like that. Everyone's taste is unique, so there's no need to judge."

"The schoolteacher look tickles my fancy," another man said.

"Whatever are you talking about?" I asked.

"Pay no heed to my gentleman friends," Cora said. "They've been enjoying your splendid spirits. Although your landlady informed me you're down to the last bottle of brandy. I trust you can rustle up more. We were hoping for a late one."

"That's what I'd like to talk to you about," I said. "I must ask you to move on."

Cora looked confused, although it was an act. She knew what I needed her to do, and from the cold glint in her eyes, she wasn't pleased.

"That makes terrible business sense," Cora said. "Why would you want to send our excellent and overly generous custom to another pub?"

"It's not just your drinking that needs to move on," I said. "Unfortunately, your room is no longer available."

"Your landlady assured me I could have the room for the entire week, and I've paid up front," Cora protested. "I shall be staying. You've no grounds to remove me."

"She's after more money," the dark-haired man muttered. "Slip her a few bob, and she'll go away."

"This has nothing to do with money," I said. "The Rusty Nail is a respectable drinking establishment."

Cora heaved out a sigh. "Which makes me think you don't consider me respectable. May I ask why?"

"The slight is not aimed at you," I replied. "But my landlady is concerned about the company you keep. I'm also unhappy you asked her to remain open after legal drinking hours. I could lose my licence over that."

"She was compensated for the inconvenience," Cora said. "Oh, I see she didn't mention I gave her money to keep the pumps running. Perhaps your dear landlady is keeping other secrets from you. If I were in charge of this pub, I'd have words."

"That's beside the point. I must ask you to gather your things and find alternative accommodation. I'm sorry if it inconveniences you, but as the owner of this pub, I have every right to request customers leave."

The men grumbled their dissatisfaction, and one of them stood as if intending to confront me, but Cora placed a hand on his arm and shook her head.

"This is a matter for two ladies to negotiate. Gentlemen, if you'll excuse me. I won't keep you waiting for long."

"There is nothing to negotiate," I said.

Cora slid around the table and stood beside me, leaning close to my ear, so close I could smell her jasmine perfume. "My dear, you seem a sensible woman, so you understand that having such a conversation in front of men who've had far too much to drink to form a coherent thought is unwise. Let's take this to my room. We can talk without interference and sort everything out."

After a second's hesitation, I admitted she had a point. The men crowded around the table were eyeing me none too kindly.

"Very well, but I won't change my mind," I said.

"I'll be back in a few moments, my darlings," Cora blew the men a kiss before sauntering off, with an exaggerated sway to her hips.

I followed with Benji beside me. I was none too happy about being bossed around in my own pub, but Cora had an air of unswerving confidence I grudgingly admired.

We ascended the stairs in silence. Cora pulled a metal key from her handbag and attempted to unlock her door. She jiggled it several times, glancing at me.

"Whilst this pub is charming, there are improvements needed. This lock isn't suitable. On more than one occasion, I've been unable to turn the key fully, so the door hasn't been secure."

"I'll get that seen to," I said. "But this area is respectable, so you've no need to fear an intruder accessing your room."

"Even so, I need more beauty sleep these days. A woman can only fend off age for so long, and my rest isn't helped by the thought someone may enter my room uninvited."

The key finally turned, and Cora pushed open the door. I stepped into the room. It was tidy, two suitcases resting at the foot of a double bed, and a scattering of cosmetics and perfumes upon the small dressing table.

Cora turned to face me. "What will it take to change your mind?"

"I must put the welfare of my staff and the reputation of my pub above all else," I said. "The company you keep is not welcome."

"Again with the slights for no reason." Cora pouted. "I've brought you business, and we spend freely. This is a pub, not an exclusive gentlemen's club. We're doing no harm."

"You may stay tonight, but you must move on tomorrow," I said. "I won't have my employees agitated. Maudie has worked for my family for years."

Cora tilted her head. "This is a family business, then? Your father is involved?"

"He was. He died."

"I'm terribly sorry. During the war?"

"That's none of your concern." I was usually content to speak of my late father, but Cora's casual confidence irritated me. She seemed so certain she would bend me to her will.

"My apologies. Losing a family member is difficult. I remember my parents' final days. They weren't easy."

A little of my irritation faded as her expression turned wistful.

"Even when we're grown, we rely on our families for so much. Alas, I have no one to rely on," Cora said. "Once my parents died, I was alone. An only child. Still, I made the best of things."

"I see from your fine clothing you've done just that," I said. "Did you make it yourself?"

"Indeed. I excel with a needle." Cora's gaze swept over my practical attire. "Don't be fooled by outward appearances. I'd have taken you for a common farmer's wife until you opened your mouth. It's important to look beneath the surface to get a true reflection of character."

Again, Cora surprised me with her astuteness. "May I ask what line of work you're in?"

A smile flickered across Cora's face. "I'm retired."

"My landlady said you wanted a room because you needed a break," I said. "Not a break from work?"

"I hate to admit it, but I feel the aches and pains of impending decrepitude creeping upon me. I thought quiet time in a quaint pub in a pleasant part of London would help me relax."

"You find it relaxing to surround yourself with drunken men each evening and drink into the early hours?"

"We all have our foibles, Miss Vale. I'm sure you're not perfect, even if you pretend to be."

"I pretend no such thing," I said.

Cora coolly appraised me for several seconds. "Let's settle this and speak of it no more."

"It is settled. I've extended the courtesy of letting you have this evening. That gives you time to make arrangements elsewhere. I believe that perfectly reasonable," I said.

Cora walked to the dressing table, picked up a small, beaded purse, and opened it. She pulled out a bundle of notes, counted several off, and held them out to me.

I stared at the money. "I thought you'd already paid in advance."

"This is a bonus for being so understanding," Cora said.

I shook my head. "I have no need of your money. I am not for bribing."

"A negotiator. I appreciate that." She pulled off three more notes, rolled them together, and stepped closer. "You could buy yourself some more practical tweed. Perhaps more walking shoes, so you can take your splendid dog out comfortably attired."

I narrowed my gaze. "Miss Bellamy, you cannot buy your way out of this situation. You've acted inappropriately, and your custom is no longer welcome at the Rusty Nail."

"I'm a generous woman, but my generosity has limits," Cora said.

"I'm happy to refund the rest of your money," I replied, "but you cannot stay."

"You're being unreasonable."

"As are you. You must understand that, if you break the rules, there are consequences."

"I hope you apply those consequences to your landlady," Cora said. "She was more than happy to remain open after hours once I slipped her money. Or do I smell the whiff of double standards?"

"I shall speak to Maudie at an appropriate time," I said.

Cora tutted and slid the notes back into her purse, snapping it shut and slapping it down on the dressing table. "Very well. I shall leave in the morning. But I hope you reconsider overnight. Perhaps, if you check the books, you'll see how profitable it is to have me and my friends frequenting the Rusty Nail. I enjoy trips all around London. If you've more pubs, I'd be happy to visit them too."

"We'll put a stop to this relationship now," I said. "It's the best for both of us."

"If you weren't so narrow-minded, you'd see sense."

"And if you behaved appropriately, we wouldn't be having this conversation. Good evening to you." I turned on my heel and marched out of the room.

Cora stamped after me. "Good evening to you, Miss Vale."

I stomped down the stairs and into the bar, with Benji right behind me.

Maudie's eyes widened as I approached. "Is there a problem?"

"I've dealt with Cora. She'll be gone in the morning. But we must have words."

Colour leeched from her face. "Give me a few minutes. I need to change a barrel or we'll have complaining customers."

I settled myself in with another gin fizz, Benji at my side, my hand resting on his head to calm my nerves. Normally, little rattled me, but after my visit to Ruby, my composure had already been tested, so even the smallest of provocations proved trying.

Ten minutes later, Maudie was back behind the bar, and Cora had rejoined her gentleman friends. Their laughter was more subdued. I was also receiving several unfriendly looks from the men, so I assumed Cora had told them they'd be moving on. They could glower and complain all they liked, but I wouldn't have the Rusty Nail used inappropriately.

After my second gin fizz, I felt mellower. I called Maudie over. "Do you have any spare rooms?"

"Yes, it's just Cora staying," she said.

"I'll sleep here overnight to monitor things," I said. "Miss Bellamy has an excessive helping of confidence, so I won't be surprised if she digs in her heels come morning. I'll be here to ensure those cases are packed and she's out the door."

"I'd appreciate that," Maudie said. "She has a way with words. I think I've got things sorted then realise we're having another lock-in, and she's invited even more friends."

"We'll talk about that too. Cora was forthright with me. It appears you weren't."

Maudie dropped her gaze and mumbled something that sounded like an apology.

"Off you go. Deal with the customers. I'll watch Cora and her crowd." I swapped my gin fizz for coffee and spent the rest of the evening soaking up the pub's atmosphere, even enjoying conversations with a few regulars. Many remembered my late father and spoke fondly of him.

The bell for last orders rang, and patrons slowly departed. Though Cora and her friends were the last to go, there were no requests for lock-ins or extra drinks. Cora kissed each gentleman in an overly friendly manner before sashaying past me, giving a small finger wave.

I helped Maudie tidy the pub then retired for the evening after making a quick telephone call home to let my mother and Matthew know where I'd be staying, so they wouldn't worry.

After washing my face, I was grateful to slip between the cool, clean sheets and quickly drifted off after what had been a hectic day.

It felt as though I hadn't been asleep five minutes before I was shaken awake.

Maudie stood over me, eyes wide.

"Is something wrong?" I asked.

"You need to come with me. Cora's dead!"

Chapter 5

After dressing as hastily as speed and decorum allowed, I dashed along the hallway to Cora's bedroom, where the door was wide open.

"Did you hear her cry out?" I asked as I approached the bed.

"No. I came to take away her late supper." Maudie remained by the door, her arms clasped about her middle, comforting herself with a hug. "Cora always has a glass of warm milk and a lettuce sandwich. She says they help her sleep. I always come up and take away her tray before I turn in. Normally, she leaves it outside the door, but it wasn't there, so I crept open the door to see if she'd forgotten."

"Her door wasn't locked?" I pressed two fingers against the pulse point on Cora's neck. All signs of life were gone.

"It was locked, but it's easy enough to jiggle open," Maudie said.

"Cora complained about the insubstantial lock," I murmured, stepping away from the body, my gaze drifting about the room. "She came up to bed alone, didn't she?"

"I think so. I didn't see her bring a gentleman up here, and we don't allow that," Maudie said.

"Given Cora's propensity for not following the rules, I wouldn't have put it past her to sneak a man up here." A quick check under the bed and in the small wardrobe confirmed there was no one else in the room, although the sash window was raised, despite the chill in the evening air, and there was a smear of mud on the sill.

I popped my head out and looked down into the alley behind the pub. There was no one lurking. I returned to the bed and carefully folded back the bedsheet.

Cora wore a beautiful nightgown edged with lace. It appeared untouched, and there were no signs of bruising on her arms, face, or neck. Nothing to suggest anyone had harmed her.

"Do you think her heart gave out?" Maudie asked. "She's a well-preserved lady, but I believe she's almost sixty."

"Gracious. Is she really?" I peered closer at Cora's face. Without the makeup, I could see she was at least ten years older than she'd appeared when we'd first met, but I wouldn't have put her anywhere near sixty.

"She always said it was down to the expensive face cream she puts on every night," Maudie said. "Some sort of cream with milk in it. It sounded vile to me."

"That, and most likely excellent bone structure," I said. "It's possible she died in her sleep. If she drinks excessively, it could have weakened her constitution."

"She was drinking every night she stayed here," Maudie said, "and she'd often take a glass of wine with her lunch, too."

"Even if this was a natural death, the police must be informed," I remarked. And that meant tangling with the most unpleasant Detective Chief Inspector Taylor. We weren't friends and had often growled at each other when Jacob served under him.

Detective Chief Inspector Taylor was an imbecile who climbed the ladder for accolades rather than to serve justice.

"I'll make the telephone call." Maudie dashed away, thumping down the stairs as she headed into the back hallway where the only telephone in the building was kept.

Benji had been pacing about the room and stopped by the wastepaper basket. He poked his nose in and sniffed before looking up at me.

I headed over to discover a few scrunched pieces of paper. One was a tissue with a lipstick blot. Another was a piece with writing, most of it illegible. But a line read: *If anything happens to me...* It was unfinished.

Was Cora concerned that her life was at risk? To whom was she writing this note? She told me she had no family, so perhaps she intended it for one of the gentlemen she'd been spending time with.

I placed the crumpled note back in the basket. I didn't want Detective Chief Inspector Taylor to accuse me of tampering.

I walked back to the window and looked outside again. I inhaled sharply. There was a figure in the shadows. I couldn't make out whether it was a man or a woman, but there would be no reason for them to stand there unless they wished to observe the goings-on in the Rusty Nail.

"Let's see what you're about, shall we?" I signalled for Benji to follow me, and we dashed down the stairs. I hurried to the main door, slid the bolt open, and gestured for Benji to head outside.

He knew what he needed to do and shot off. A few seconds later, there came a scrambling of feet and a yelp.

I stepped outside the pub, surprised by the sharp chill in the air. It was even less reason for Cora to have had her bedroom window open, unless she'd been feeling unwell. If she'd had a fever, she'd have welcomed the chilliness.

Maudie hurried over to join me. "I've told the police what's going on, and they're on their way. What are you doing out in the cold?"

"Someone was watching the pub," I said. "I sent Benji after them."

"Whoever would be out so late?"

"Perhaps the person who is associated with Cora's lack of pulse."

There was a second of silence. "Oh, my word!" Maudie clutched her chest and staggered towards the bar. "Do you think this was murder?"

I hurried to her side. "We must consider all possibilities. Take deep breaths. It's always a shock when you find a body."

Maudie sucked in several breaths, bent over double, one hand on her knee. "It's my first body. Well, I saw my parents off, of course, but that's not the same thing. Finding someone dead, one of your guests, it's a shock."

"Would you like a brandy?" I asked. "I find it settles the nerves."

"Thank you." Maudie drew in a shaky breath. "But I'll fetch it."

"You take a seat and recover yourself." I pushed her firmly onto a stool. I knew my way around a bar.

A few minutes later, we were settled on stools, drinking brandy. Benji had yet to return. Our lurker must be swift on their feet or have a handy hiding spot if Benji hadn't caught them and dragged them back.

"Remind me how long Cora had been here before you contacted me with your concerns?" I asked.

"Just a few days." Maudie looked into her brandy.

"She said she'd paid upfront for her stay."

"Yes, she did. She always paid in advance."

"Always? So, she's been here before?"

"No! I mean, she paid in advance this time. It's unusual. Normally, people settle the bill at the end of their stay. But she paid for her room up front in cash."

"She seemed to be a wealthy woman," I said. "And she attempted to bribe me into allowing her to stay. There were plenty of notes in her purse."

"Did you accept her offer?" Maudie asked.

"Unlike you, I turned her down."

Maudie gulped down a mouthful of brandy, making herself cough. "She told you?"

"As I mentioned, Cora was forthright with me. She said you'd been well paid to ensure the lock-ins went smoothly."

"I'm ever so sorry," Maudie said. "I saw no harm. Now and again, me and the regulars have a lock-in. I thought it would be the same with Cora and her friends, but they were much rowdier. They kept insisting on the most expensive whisky and brandy, and they expected table service. It was humiliating. And they stayed later than they were supposed to. One evening, they were here until almost dawn. I was dead on my feet."

"Do I not pay you enough? Is that why you need the extra money?" I asked.

"Your pay is more generous than anyone's around here," Maudie said. "I didn't think. I won't do it again. Please don't sack me."

"Let's have no talk like that," I said. "You're excellent at your job, and I don't want to lose you, but we can't have this sort of thing happening. The occasional lock-in with the regulars you trust, I'll overlook. But having strangers in here, ordering you about and inconveniencing you so the business suffers, is inappropriate."

"It'll never happen again," Maudie said. "When I realised what a problem Cora was, that was when I got in touch with you. It was time for her to go. No amount of money is worth that trouble."

There was a scratching at the door, and I hurried to open it. Benji appeared. He was alone.

"Oh, bad luck. Don't tell me our lurker escaped?"

He whined and lifted one paw.

"Never mind, old boy. Perhaps you're slowing down. It happens to the best of us."

He harrumphed softly, as if not liking that idea one bit.

"Fear not. If they're important to this puzzle, we'll winkle them out and deal with them," I said. I was about to close the door when two cars zoomed along the quiet road.

"That'll be the police." Maudie had joined me and was peering out.

Benji growled softly as Detective Chief Inspector Taylor emerged from the passenger seat. Of course, he considered himself far too grand to drive himself here. Three uniformed officers accompanied him, and they marched towards the pub.

Detective Chief Inspector Taylor scowled when he recognised me. "Why is it that I always find you in the middle of all of our local deaths, Miss Vale?"

"That statement is entirely untrue," I said. "Working at the London Times, I'm well aware of the number of deaths that occur around here, and I'm involved in barely any of them."

Detective Chief Inspector Taylor adjusted his tie, his scowl deepening. "Pubs always bring trouble, and yours most of all. Stand aside and let us see what we're dealing with."

"Allow me to show you the scene," I said.

"The scene of what, exactly?" Detective Chief Inspector Taylor asked. "The telephone call we received said a woman had most likely died in her sleep. Who telephoned in the death?"

"That would be me, sir." Maudie lifted a shaking hand. "I found Miss Bellamy dead in her bed. I didn't know what to think had happened to her."

"It was most likely a heart attack. You told me she was elderly."

"You shouldn't make assumptions, Detective Chief Inspector," I said. "Not until you've viewed the scene."

"I could say the same for you," he said. "Calling anything a scene suggests suspicious activity. You leave this to me and my men. You, show me the body." He pointed at Maudie. "And you," he pointed at me, "wait outside."

"This is my pub!" I said.

"Which means you'll appreciate us working swiftly, so we don't have to close it for weeks and you lose business. Sergeant, wait with Miss Vale and ensure she comes to no harm or causes any mischief."

"I must protest," I said. "I need to know what's going on in my own establishment."

Detective Chief Inspector Taylor sighed. "And when I have a moment to inform you, I will. But while you stand in my way, all hoity-toity, you're obstructing justice. Which means I could have you arrested. Do you want my sergeant to put you in handcuffs and sit you in the back of the car?"

I was tempted to see if he'd carry out his threat, but I didn't particularly want to spend the night in prison. After glaring at Detective Chief Inspector Taylor for several seconds, and him doing likewise, I stepped outside the pub.

"Good girl. You see sense at last. This way, men." Detective Chief Inspector Taylor led the charge, with Maudie showing them the way.

"Good girl," I growled under my breath. "I'm not some well-behaved dog who deserves a pat on the head for obeying her master."

The tall, round-faced sergeant who remained with me chuckled then stopped when I glared at him. "Sorry, Miss. It's just that you have a reputation at the station. Detective Chief Inspector Taylor complained about you the entire way here. He said he hoped it wasn't one of your pubs, because you always get in the way and embarrass him."

"The man is already a fool, so it's a simple matter to point out his foibles," I said. "I don't believe we've met before." I held out my hand.

He took it. "I feel like I know you, even though we've never met. I'm Sergeant Redcote. I'm good friends with Sergeant Matthers, and he speaks highly of you. He said you helped him with difficult murder cases."

"Sergeant Matthers is an excellent fellow," I said. "I haven't seen him recently. How is he doing?"

"He was wounded in the line of duty, Miss," Sergeant Redcote said. "He's been off work for three weeks, just come back on duty."

"Gracious, I had no idea. I'll have to tell Jacob, too. They worked closely together when he was in the police."

"Would that be Jacob Templeton?"

"Indeed, it is. After his injury, we went into business together. He runs my private investigation agency in Kent."

"I heard all about that from Sergeant Matthers. That sounds like exciting work."

"It has its moments," I said. "The business is thriving. It seems there are always scandals and troubles that need fixing, no matter what part of the country you live in."

"Give my regards to Mr Templeton," Sergeant Redcote said. "He had one of the best records for solving murders in this district."

"I suspect a little of that was down to my assistance," I said with a smile. "But I shall pass on your regards." I looked back at the pub and peered up at the window, wondering how long Detective Chief Inspector Taylor would linger.

Someone softly cleared their throat, and I turned, hoping to see the lurker had returned. It was far worse than that.

"Isabella Micheals! What in blue blazes are you doing here?" I asked, forgetting my manners.

Isabella, rival journalist and the cruel woman who broke my brother's heart, smirked and sauntered towards me. "Catching the scoop of the century, it would seem. I didn't know you ran brothels these days."

Chapter 6

"Brothels? As usual, you're speaking nonsense." I turned away from Isabella. "What are you doing out at such a late hour? Chasing some gutter story to sell for a few pennies, I suppose?"

"I go where the stories are, and this is quite some story." Isabella moved closer, her eyes gleaming in the gloom. She nodded a greeting to Sergeant Redcote.

"There's no story here." I refused to look at her. "Go home."

"My sources say otherwise," Isabella replied. "Or will you deny there's a body inside your pub?"

I cast her a glare from the corner of my eye. "How would you know that?"

"Sources. The same as you. I'm friendly with a few policemen at the local station. They pass on the interesting titbits."

"What favours do you offer to ensure that happens?" I regretted the sharpness of my tone, but Isabella irritated me, and I'd never forgiven her for the way she treated Matthew.

"There's no need to be unpleasant," Isabella said. "Policemen get paid little, so a Christmas hamper or a bottle of whisky and a friendly smile does a lot to convince a man to talk. Don't you agree?"

"I couldn't say," I replied. "I keep my relationships professional."

"Always the perfect one, aren't you? But we all have our ways of achieving the same ends," Isabella said. "Don't you want to learn about the dead woman inside your pub? I imagine Detective Chief Inspector Taylor has been less than forthcoming with information. Kicked you out of your own pub, has he?"

"What information do you claim to have?" I asked, curious despite my annoyance. "You mentioned something about a brothel."

"Do you not know the notorious Cora Bellamy?" Isabella asked.

"She's not notorious to me," I said. "I've never met the woman until tonight."

"Because you stay away from the seedier parts of society," Isabella said. "That's where some of the most magnificent stories are found."

"Stop bragging and tell me the information or leave," I said.

"I'll share if you do," Isabella said after a pause.

"I've very little to share."

"Did you meet Cora before she died?"

I hesitated and then nodded. "I did."

"And had you formed an opinion of her?" Isabella asked. "From your tone, I assume it was unfavourable."

"She wasn't the right customer for the Rusty Nail."

"And why would that be? Because she preferred the company of gentlemen over women?"

"What does that have to do with anything?" I asked.

Isabella grinned. "I'm having too much fun, but I'll spill. Cora Bellamy ran one of the most exclusive brothels in Belgravia."

"What nonsense," I said. "She's a retired genteel lady. She came to the pub to calm her nerves."

"Hah! I think it's far more likely she came to this part of London to escape a troubling situation connected to her role as a society madam," Isabella said.

I took a moment to consider the possibility. From my brief meeting with Cora, I'd realised she was concealing her true intentions. But a brothel madam? Surely not.

"Cora was escaping a difficult situation," Isabella whispered.

"Was someone chasing her?" I asked, my attention fully on Isabella.

"Find the answer to that, and you'll likely find the person who ended Cora's life."

I sniffed, still unsure whether to trust Isabella. "The police are investigating what happened. They're not even sure any foul play was involved."

"You are, though," Isabella said. "What did you see that caught your interest?"

I looked back at the pub. At first glance, nothing had seemed amiss in Cora's room, but the more I observed, the less certain I was that her death had been from natural causes.

"I've shared the information I have about Cora. It's only fair you do the same about the crime scene," Isabella said.

"I'm assuming this will be on the record?"

"Naturally. Imagine the look on my employer's face when I break this story." Glee resonated in Isabella's tone. "I'll be done with those boring articles about village fetes and weddings. My name will be on the front page. Breaking a scandal like this will be the making of me. It could be for you too, though you'll need to let me publish first, but you can follow up the next day in the London Times."

I snorted. "Let's not get ahead of ourselves."

"I know that look, Veronica. We've been acquaintances for years, so I recognise when you think something is amiss. Was the murder weapon left behind? Evidence of violence? Theft?"

"From what I saw, there was no obvious murder weapon," I said somewhat grudgingly. "My landlady, Maudie, discovered Cora dead in her bed when she went to retrieve her supper tray."

"What about signs of a struggle?" Isabella asked.

I glanced at Sergeant Redcote, who listened intently. "Cora appeared untouched. I was careful when I checked the body. Her nightgown hadn't been disturbed, and there were no marks or bruises on her skin."

Isabella faced the pub. "Cora's business catered to an elite clientele. Businessmen of high standing, politicians, even minor members of the Royal Family. She kept her client base exclusive so she could charge more. But that made her vulnerable. These men demanded silence and a guarantee that they would never be associated with Cora's brothel. The scandal would have ruined them."

"You're suggesting Cora wasn't as discreet as she ought to have been?" I asked.

"I don't believe she was," Isabella said. "And that indiscretion caused her to flee from the brothel and hide here. I'm not sure what her long-term plan was, but whoever realised she was up to no good came after her."

"When I looked around her room, I found a crumpled note," I said. "It was as if she was writing a warning or a message in case anything happened to her, but then changed her mind."

"There you go! Proof positive that Cora knew her life was in danger," Isabella said. "She must have spoken to the wrong person, and word got back to a man of influence."

"If any of what you're saying is true, chaps like that would have no qualms about silencing a woman like Cora."

"They'd have no respect for a lady who ran such a business. They'd pretend to, but they were there for one purpose." There was a trace of bitterness in Isabella's voice. "Once they get what they want, they discard the women like yesterday's fish and chip paper."

"It's a dreadful business but a profitable one for Cora," I said. "And one I fear she carried on once she'd settled here."

Isabella arched an eyebrow. "Go on."

"I was here this evening because my landlady was concerned about Cora's behaviour. There have been several parties involving men."

"My, my. I was right all along," Isabella said. "You have been running a brothel from the Rusty Nail."

"Take those words out of your mouth! It's absolutely untrue," I snapped. "The Rusty Nail is a respectable pub. I would never permit such activities to take place."

"Maybe you wouldn't. But what about your landlady?" Isabella asked.

"Maudie is honest." I drew in a breath and frowned. She hadn't been honest with me. She'd taken money from Cora to hold exclusive lock-ins. Had she lied about other things?

"What else did you see in the room that piqued your suspicions?" Isabella asked. "It can't just have been a crumpled note."

"The door lock is faulty," I said. "It's possible someone gained access after Cora retired for the night."

"Anything else?"

"The window was open. It's only a single flight down, so someone agile and prepared to take a risk could have gained access or jumped out after committing the crime. And someone was watching the pub. Benji gave chase, but they got away."

"That's most unlike the fine Benji to let a criminal escape." Isabella reached over and scratched the top of Benji's head.

"They must be fast and fit to elude Benji," I agreed.

"Was it the killer watching to make sure they'd completed the job?"

"Some criminals like to stay close to the crime scene and watch the chaos unfold," I said.

"Or perhaps they were worried they'd left behind incriminating evidence," Isabella said. "They were hoping to get back inside, but your landlady discovered the body before they had the opportunity."

"That is also a possibility," I admitted.

"And what about your landlady?" Isabella asked. "Do you have concerns about her?"

I discreetly chewed my bottom lip. Maudie was one of the last people to see Cora alive. She'd also been unhappy with the way Cora behaved. And she'd served her a meal before she went to sleep. What if she put something in Cora's food? The glass of milk was still on the nightstand. Would Maudie have been so callous?

"You're hiding something," Isabella said. "This partnership won't work if we conceal things."

"There is no partnership," I said. "We can both publish a story about this murder. I'm not greedy."

Isabella narrowed her gaze. "I'm content to share, provided I publish first."

"How gracious of you," I said. "But I have no more information to share."

"You will continue to let me know when new information shows up, though?" Isabella asked. "It's the only way I'll get my name on a byline. You know what these stuffed shirts in newspapers are like. They can't abide a woman being smarter than they are."

I sighed but nodded. It was a frustration we shared. As women in a previously all-male profession, we struggled to gain recognition. I'd had a slightly easier time of it than Isabella, thanks to my uncle, but he never gave me an easy ride.

"I have an idea," Isabella said. "We need to go to the Belgravia Club and speak to the girls. It has a new madam, so it's still open."

"Those ladies will never speak to us," I said.

"*I* won't be the issue. But if you go there alone, your primness will terrify them." Isabella laughed. "And I can't remember the last time I saw you smile."

"I've had a lot to deal with recently."

"Oh! It's not Matthew, is it?"

I pressed my lips together. "Do you suppose they'll talk to you?"

"I have a way of getting people to open up," Isabella said. "Although I know who would be perfect for this assignment. Your friend, Ruby. I haven't seen her around lately. I suppose she's found herself a charming young man who's swept her off her feet. But she's exactly who we need. A pretty face and a curvy figure would fit in at the club. We could get her in under the guise of a potential—"

"That won't be possible," I said. "Ruby is... indisposed."

"Indisposed? How indisposed?"

"As in it's none of your business indisposed," I retorted.

"You two haven't fallen out, have you?" Isabella asked. "You're the best of friends."

"And we still are," I said. "But Ruby won't be going to any tawdry club, and neither will I."

"Then you'll miss out," Isabella said. "With Cora gone, the Belgravia Club's future will be in peril. The girls will be worried. Worried people make errors."

"Or they'll have their guards up and their lips closed," I said. The idea of speaking to the women Cora had employed was tempting, and it irked me that Isabella had thought of it first. "Isn't it time you went home? Your mother will be worrying about you."

"I can be out as late as I desire." Isabella lifted her chin, a familiar fire of indignation lighting her gaze.

"How is she doing?" I'd visited Isabella's mother not so long ago and discovered she was gravely ill.

"Things are much the same," Isabella said, the fire fading. "She had a rough time over the winter, but she's stable. I'm staying with her for as long as needed." Isabella looked at me. "I... I saw Matthew the other day."

"When did you see him?" I instantly stiffened.

"He was walking a dog. An adorable little thing."

"That would be Felix," I said. "They've been good for each other."

"He looked well. Better. Is he better?"

"Matthew will never fully recover from his wartime experiences, so don't get yourself tangled up with him again," I warned her.

"I didn't mean that," Isabella said, flushing. "I just wanted to know how he was doing. He's a sweet man."

"Yes, well... you really should be going. If the police see you lurking for much longer, they'll ask questions." I glared pointedly at Sergeant Redcote, who still listened in.

Isabella's gaze dropped to the ground. "I meant no harm by asking about Matthew. We were once dreadfully fond of each other."

"Until you broke his heart and abandoned him when he needed you most. Good evening, Miss Michaels."

She sighed and turned away. "Good evening, Veronica. I'll be in touch about our trip to Belgravia."

Chapter 7

"Pass the marmalade." My mother sat upright in her bed, a fringed shawl around her shoulders, covering her nightgown. Matthew and I perched at the bottom of the bed in comfortable positions, pillows tucked behind us so the metal bed rail didn't dig in.

"That's your fourth slice of toast!" I said.

"And that's your third," Matthew retorted.

"I walk Benji for at least two hours a day, so I need the energy," I said.

"I need energy to look after those kittens you've foisted upon us." My mother tucked into her marmalade smeared slice of toast. "They kept me up half the night with their meowing."

"They were in Matthew's room," I said. "How on earth did you hear them?"

"For a woman of my advanced years, I have excellent hearing," my mother said. "And you should be grateful for my hearty appetite. Most people my age eat like sparrows and wither away whenever they catch so much as a cold."

"We've no fear of that," I said.

"What's with the sharpness?" Matthew asked.

I sighed. "My apologies. I slept little last night, thinking about all the goings-on at the Rusty Nail."

"Haven't you got that figured out by now?" Matthew said. "You enjoy solving these puzzles."

I set down my cup of tea. "This one is a conundrum. Perhaps I'm making this more complicated than it needs to be. Cora could have simply died in her sleep."

"I suppose you won't find out much from the police now that Jacob is no longer in charge," my mother said.

"That is a tricky issue. I still have Sergeant Matthers, and I made a new acquaintance last night. Sergeant Redcote. He seems to think well of me."

"You're too busy to poke around in another mystery," my mother said. "Although, keep us informed. I need to tell the neighbours what's going on. None of us sleep when we know a heartless killer is striding around London."

"Perish the thought you don't have the latest gossip to spread." I winced. My sharp tongue had unfurled again. It didn't help that my head throbbed with tiredness. I'd tossed and turned all night, wondering about Cora's death. "If the kittens become too troublesome, I'll have them collected by a volunteer from the dogs' home."

"Oh, they can stay for another week or so." My mother waved her hand in my general direction. "So long as they don't bother Felix."

"Felix loves them," Matthew said. "He'd like it if I took them out on walks with us, but can you imagine the chaos if I did?"

I speared him with a stern glance. "Speaking of walks, have you met anyone interesting while you've been out?"

He shrugged. "No one comes to mind. You know me. I'm not keen on speaking to strangers."

"No nice young ladies you consider of interest?"

Matthew's cheeks flushed. "I don't have time for that. Besides, who would have me?"

I narrowed my gaze. "What about Isabella Michaels? I hope you've been nowhere near her."

"That dreadful woman!" my mother exclaimed. "After everything she did to you."

"She did nothing to me," Matthew muttered. "I did it to myself. You know I wasn't right after serving. I can't expect a woman like Isabella to wait for some wretched creature who stuttered every time he spoke and couldn't meet anyone's gaze."

"You've made excellent progress without interference from Isabella," I said. "Much of that is thanks to Felix. He's an excellent dog. Almost as excellent as Benji."

Benji and Felix lingered by the bed, knowing there'd soon be leftover breakfast heading their way. Their ears had pricked when I said their names.

"Does that mean you met Isabella?" my mother asked.

"We bumped into each other," Matthew said. "She was walking in one direction, and I was going towards the park. I could hardly ignore her."

"You should have," I said. "Isabella hasn't changed. Her only interest is her career. That's why she was hanging about outside the Rusty Nail last night. She has an inside source at the police who tipped her off."

"I've learnt my lesson," Matthew said. "It's a bachelor's life for me."

Mother sighed. "I shall never have grandchildren. Veronica is too focussed on dashing around and putting herself in danger. And you're only interested in... well, I'm not entirely sure what you're interested in."

"Matthew has hobbies!" I said. "We mustn't be hard on him. But take care, especially around women as wily as Isabella. She still considers you sweet."

He wrinkled his nose. "That's a compliment?"

"Ignore her. And if you see her again, turn around and walk the other way." I popped the last of my toast into my mouth before feeding a crust to Benji. "Now, I must be off. I need to get back to the Rusty Nail and see what mess the police have left. And I intend to talk to Maudie."

"After what you told us about her, you should sack her," my mother said. "Taking money from a woman like Cora Bellamy. It's a scandal!"

"I want her to be open with me, so sacking her before we've spoken would be unhelpful." I stood and gently shook toast crumbs from my skirt, which the dogs consumed. "Maudie has always been a hard worker, and until yesterday, I thought she was honest. Perhaps I've been deceived. Or Cora was lying."

Mother harrumphed. "If I weren't counting down to my final breath, I'd sort her out."

I exchanged an amused look with Matthew. "I'll bring home a fish and chip supper, shall I?"

My mother rubbed her hands together. "Now I've got something to look forward to. It'll keep me alive that bit longer."

I discreetly rolled my eyes before exiting the bedroom, collecting my handbag, sliding into my shoes, and heading out to work. I was only popping in to show my face and ensure the men didn't grumble about me not doing my duty, but Uncle Harry would want me to investigate the death at the Rusty Nail. He wouldn't give me the story, but I could get useful information to make for an exciting headline.

After a brisk walk to the office with Benji, I hurried in, ignoring the men's icy stares, checked the pile of obituaries I needed to go through, and then dashed into Uncle Harry's office.

He was already deep in his work, his shirt sleeves rolled up and his tie flung over his shoulder. He looked up with a distracted expression. "I already know what you're going to say. You have obligations here."

"I'll take my obituaries with me. I can work on them at the Rusty Nail. I won't miss the deadline."

"Is there anyone influential in your pile of death notices who needs more time spent on them than usual?" Uncle Harry leant back in his seat and tilted his head from side to side to ease a tight neck.

"They'll all receive the appropriate attention," I replied, "but I must get to the bottom of what happened at the Rusty Nail."

"If the rumours are true, you've been conducting less-than-legal business there."

"I think, sadly, they are true, but it has nothing to do with me," I said. "Which is why I need to get back there swiftly. I must know how much damage has been done. I'm at risk of losing my licence."

Uncle Harry winced. "We can't have that. You do what you need to do, but I want all of those obituaries written up by the end of the day. No excuses."

"You never get them from me." I dashed around his desk, pressed a kiss to his cheek, and then hurried out again.

I hopped onto the number forty-two bus that would take me on the half-hour journey to the Rusty Nail. I selected the top deck, where it was quiet, so I could work on my first two obituaries. One was for a gentleman who'd met a sticky end after poking his finger into a socket that shouldn't have been poked. The other was an elderly lady who had lived a long and fabulous life, but then slipped on a patch of oil and died in a rather undignified fashion upside down, revealing her undergarments to all.

With those obituaries outlined, I hopped off the bus as it arrived at the stop closest to the Rusty Nail and walked briskly with Benji to the front door. It was locked, but there was no sign of any police, so I knocked and waited for Maudie to open it. She appeared a moment later, looking rather frazzled around the edges, her eyes red-rimmed, suggesting she'd slept as little as I had.

She gestured me in and closed the door. "Have you eaten?" "At home," I said. "Although I'd welcome a cup of coffee." "I'm just finishing up in the back. Come through." Maudie was still in her dressing gown with curlers in her hair. "How long did the police keep you up?" I settled at her small kitchen table in the private rooms that came as part of the job.

"They were here till gone three," Maudie said. "Went all over the bedroom. Then they waited for the doctor to arrive and look at the body before Cora was taken. They also spoke to me. I hope I said everything I should."

I sipped the steaming cup of coffee Maudie had given me. "Did you know Cora's line of work when you accepted her as a guest at the Rusty Nail?"

Maudie fiddled with the salt and pepper shakers on the table, a half-finished breakfast sitting beside her. "I had an idea. I haven't always been in the pub trade. I used to clean for various gentlemen. Mainly bachelors. They're a messy bunch, always leaving their clothes and towels scattered around."

"That was how you met Cora?" I asked. "I never met her, but I heard about her," Maudie said. "These gentlemen were well-to-do. They liked to entertain and take their friends to places where they could enjoy the company of... ladies."

"You don't need to be polite about it," I said. "Cora Bellamy ran a brothel in Belgravia."

"Oh! How do you know that?" Maudie asked. "Through my connections," I said. "I wasn't aware of who she was when I met her last night, but you knew, and you still allowed her to stay here."

Maudie shifted in her seat. "I... I haven't been completely honest." "As I'm discovering." I set down my cup and stared at her, unblinking. "Tell me everything."

Maudie gulped. "I'm scared to. I love my job. It gives me so much freedom. I can't afford to lose it." "You should have thought about that before you acted recklessly," I said. "Let's get our cards on the table and be truthful. Leave nothing out."

Maudie's shoulders slumped. "This isn't the first time Cora has stayed here. Occasionally, she would visit with a gentleman because she needed a discreet place for a few hours."

"She conducted her business in this pub?" My nostrils flared as my anger rose. "I never saw a thing!" Maudie said. "But having worked for those single gentlemen, I was aware of what they paid some women to do. I could tell what Cora was up to."

"I assume she paid you handsomely to use our rooms. Does that money appear in the Rusty Nail's books?"

"The money for a regular nightly reservation went into the books. You lost nothing," Maudie said.

"But you pocketed the rest?" I asked. "Cora gave you more money to ensure you remained silent?"

Maudie looked away. "She did. I shouldn't have done it, but I needed the money." "You should have found it another way," I said. "Do you not realise the risk you've put this pub under? Not to mention the entire business. My licence could be revoked. That would mean all the pubs under the Vale name would close. We'd lose everything."

"I didn't realise it was so serious." Maudie's bottom lip wobbled. "That won't happen, will it?"

"That decision is outside of my control and all because of your negligent behaviour," I said.

"I am sorry. I shouldn't have done it."

I took a few seconds to control my anger to ensure I didn't lash out too viciously. "How long has this business arrangement been going on?" "A year," she said. "Cora would visit once a month with the same gentleman." "You've been profiting off illegal activity all this time?" "Yes! But I had a good reason." "Greed is never good," I said. "You told me Cora arrived to spend a week here, resting and recovering. Was that a lie?" "She said she needed a break, but then she got an offer she couldn't refuse," Maudie said. "One of her former clients recognised her and suggested a party with some of his friends."

"So, Cora has been here for some time, running her brothel services, and you've been paid to keep quiet."

"I'm not proud of this," Maudie said, "and I am sorry if it gets you in trouble."

Maudie looked genuinely downcast, but I struggled to find sympathy for her. She'd used this business to make money through illegal means. A business my father built up from nothing. A business he was so proud of. If he were alive, it would break his heart to learn this was going on under one of his roofs.

"Take me back to last night," I said.

Maudie startled at the change of topic. "What about it?" "You were possibly one of the last people to see Cora alive. Was there anything about her that appeared odd to you? Did she seem nervous or unsettled? Did she mention anything that concerned her?" "She was her usual self," Maudie said. "She seemed tired, though. But why wouldn't she, when she's been entertaining all week?"

"She said nothing to you out of the ordinary?" "When I took her up her supper, she thanked me, and I left. That was the last time I saw her until I went to collect her supper things," Maudie said.

"What exactly did you prepare for Cora?" "A glass of warm milk with a teaspoon of sugar and a lettuce sandwich, thickly buttered. She requested the same thing every night." "You made it yourself?" "That time of night, there's no one else to help," Maudie said. "Why do you want to know?"

"Because the more I learn about Cora Bellamy, the more certain I am that her death was no accident. I'm hopeful the police will come to the same conclusion and launch an investigation to discover who murdered her."

Maudie jerked back in her seat. "You mentioned murder last night." "From the information I've gathered, Cora was in trouble. She was staying at the Rusty Nail not because she needed a break, but because she needed a refuge. Someone was after her. She'd made a mistake and got herself in trouble. Perhaps whoever it was tracked her here."

"But she was in her locked room, alone," Maudie said. "When I left her supper things, there was no one with her." "True enough. But the lock on her door is unreliable. Her window was also open. It's possible either route was used to gain entrance or exit."

Maudie's eyes widened. "Who would do such a thing?" "Before we discover that, we need to determine how they killed her," I said. "Which is why I'm so interested in the food you served. Could someone have tampered with it?" "You think someone slipped something into her food? That's impossible."

"You didn't leave the kitchen?"

Maudie paused. "For a moment. There was a noise out front. I went to check, and someone had knocked over a flowerpot, ruining all the flowers. I thought it was a drunk who had lost his balance and grabbed it. But the doors were locked in front and back, so no one could have got in to do anything to the food."

"Are the locks as flimsy as the one on Cora's door?"

Maudie winced. "The back one could be better. I've been meaning to see to it. I'm certain no one snuck in, though. I'd have heard them."

"Well, if no one snuck in..." I raised my eyebrows and stared at her, waiting for her to catch up.

Maudie gasped, and her hand slapped against her chest. "You can't think it was me."

"If the police conclude Cora was murdered, they'll consider the same thing," I said. "Perhaps you changed your mind about being bribed. You contacted me desperate to make Cora leave. You wanted her business out of the pub because you feared losing your job when you realised how serious the situation had become. I arrived and failed to remove Cora, so you took matters into your own hands."

"Never! I would never kill someone." Maudie stood from her seat, her hands clenched beside her. "I was unhappy with Cora taking advantage of me, but I wouldn't want the lady dead."

"Do you have an alibi?" "I don't need one." "What did you do after you served the supper?" "I went to my room. I was exhausted." Maudie lurched forward and grabbed my hand. "Please. It wasn't me. I've made a mistake, and I'll hold my hands up to that, but I'd never kill anybody. I desperately needed that money for my sister, you see." "Why does your sister need money?" I asked. "She's my older sister and needs care, but I can't provide it for her and work. She needs a live-in nurse, and they don't come cheap. The poor dear has been in and out of hospital over the last year, and each time she gets frailer. I can't lose her. I need the money to pay for full-time care."

"So, when Cora arrived and suggested an arrangement, it was an opportunity you couldn't refuse?"

Maudie nodded. "I never thought through the trouble it would cause you, and I never thought it would come to this."

My anger faded somewhat. People did foolish and desperate things to support loved ones. "I am sorry for the situation you find yourself in with your sister. That must be dreadfully hard."

"But don't you see? That's why I wouldn't kill Cora. She gave me enough money to pay for my sister's nurse. With Cora dead, I'm back where I was. I won't be able to help my sister. She won't last long without someone looking after her."

Although Maudie had no alibi, she made a valid point about wanting to keep her golden goose alive.

"Make sure you're prepared for when the police speak to you," I said. "Be calm and logical. Hide nothing from them. And be sure to tell them everything about your sick sister."

A choked gasp escaped Maudie, and her eyes filled with tears. "If I hadn't allowed Cora here, none of this would have happened."

"We find ourselves in an unfortunate situation, but we'll make the best of things." I extracted my hand from hers.

"What about my job?" Maudie asked. "I know I've no right to ask, and I've done wrong by you, but if I lose this job, then I'll lose all hope of looking after my sister."

"Then you need to make amends and help me find Cora's killer fast," I said. "Do you have any idea who did this?"

For a second, Maudie looked bewildered, then her eyes brightened. "I know the woman you need to speak to."

Chapter 8

With the name Iris Dane supplied by Maudie, who also revealed Iris used to work for Cora and had attended a late-night gathering at the Rusty Nail, I had a new lead.

Maudie also knew exactly where the woman worked. Iris had established a respectable hairdressing salon in Soho. I was overdue for a haircut, so I decided to visit and see what I could find out.

Soho is in the West End of London, an area I seldom frequent. It used to be a fashionable spot, but the gentry had mostly moved to the popular area of Mayfair. Pubs and restaurants were establishing themselves locally.

I parked on a quiet street nearby and took Benji for a brisk walk before heading towards the shops and locating the salon. The exterior appeared tidy, and it was clearly busy, which suggested a good quality of service.

I opened the door, and a waft of setting lotion and sweet hair tonic made my eyes water. Although I kept my hair tidy, I never relished the primping and preening that accompanied the quest for lustrous locks. There was scarcely any point in keeping my hair smart, as walking with Benji in the often-inclement

British weather invariably rearranged the style into electrocuted hedge witch.

A young, heavily made-up woman stood behind a neat reception area near a row of helmet dryers. She smiled brightly. "Do you have an appointment, miss?"

"I was hoping you could fit me in," I said. "This salon came highly recommended."

"That's good to hear." The young woman consulted the book before her. "If you don't mind waiting ten minutes, we'll have someone for you."

"Iris Dane was recommended," I said.

"Then you're in luck. That's who's available. Please take a seat. Would you like some refreshments while you wait?"

I gladly accepted a cup of coffee, and the woman returned a moment later with coffee and biscuits for me, and a bowl of water and a biscuit for Benji.

I thanked her then settled in, pretending to read a magazine while I discreetly scanned the salon. It was busy, with chairs occupied by ladies in various stages of coiffure or crimping. Some sat beneath the dryers, their hair set in curlers. One lady's head was covered in a strong-smelling dye hidden under a floppy cap.

Everything appeared neat and professional, and business was thriving. Women had always taken great care with their appearance during the Great War. Many people considered keeping themselves respectable and in tip-top condition their patriotic duty.

I'd been too occupied for that, though when I'd attended a dance, I'd attempted to look presentable. It was the least one could do for the men who gave up so much for this country.

"Iris is ready for you now." The receptionist approached me with an oversized dark gown, which she carefully helped me into and tied at the back. She led me to a comfortable chair before a large mirror, ensured I had everything I needed, and left me to it. Benji curled up contentedly at my feet.

I didn't have to wait long for Iris to arrive. She was a short, curvaceous, dark-haired woman of around thirty, with large, kohl-rimmed eyes and a thin mouth painted a vivid hue.

"I've not seen you in here before," Iris said by way of greeting.

"It's my first time," I replied. "I was lamenting to a friend that I needed a freshening up, and she suggested I come here."

"Who would that be, then?" Iris was studying my hair rather than my face.

"Mary Brown." I plucked the first invented name out of the air.

Iris's gaze flicked to mine, her eyes narrowing slightly. "Don't know her. She's not one of mine. What do you have in mind?"

"I'm no expert on hair. That's why I'm here," I said.

"You'd suit a shorter style. I take it you do a fair bit of walking?" She glanced at Benji.

"We're always out and about," I said. "A practical style would be welcome."

"Your hair is thick and has a natural curl. I can work with that. Let's get you washed, and then we'll get to work."

"Perhaps just a trim this time," I suggested.

"You said you wanted a freshen up. Then you need to go more dramatic. Short hair is very fashionable."

I hesitated. The things I did in the name of justice. "Very well. Short it is."

Ten minutes later, I sat with a towel wrapped about my wet hair, waiting for Iris to return. She'd been checking on a lady beneath a dryer, but when she saw me back in the seat, she hurried over. Unleashing a pair of sharp scissors, she set them down, unwrapped my hair, and combed it through.

"Your style suggests country living rather than city life," Iris said.

"I'm a London girl through and through," I said. "Although I don't live close to Soho. I work more centrally."

"Not surprising. Few people do unless you're in a particular trade." She sectioned my hair, pinning some on top of my head so she could work on the lower layers. "It can't be this salon that's brought you to Soho, surely?"

"Well, I am conducting a bit of business, too," I replied.

"What would that be?" From Iris's half-bored tone, I could tell she was using her usual hairdresser's patter as she focussed on my hair.

"I wear many hats," I said. "I write obituaries for a newspaper. I also run a private investigation firm in Kent with my partner, and I have a number of pubs in the area that I manage."

This information caught Iris's attention. She paused in her cutting, surprised. "I'm amazed you have time for it all. Or the ability. No offence. I always appreciate a working woman, but those are men's jobs."

"The war changed so much," I said.

"Tell me about it," Iris grumbled.

"You're finding business is struggling?"

"Business in the salon is fine," Iris said. "We've only been running for six months, and we're booked solid most days. You're lucky I had a cancellation this morning, else you'd have had to wait weeks."

"Then it really is my lucky day," I said. "Now that the war is over, I'm finding the pubs are thriving again. People enjoy being out and sociable once more."

"I'll agree with that," said Iris. "Lean forward for me."

I did as instructed. "Although I've had a spot of bad luck recently. I own the Rusty Nail, and a patron just died there."

The sound of snipping ceased. I looked up to find Iris glaring at me.

"Is something the matter?" I asked.

"You work for a newspaper. You run a private investigation firm, and you own the pub where Cora Bellamy died."

"That's correct. Did you know Cora?"

Iris set down her scissors and folded her arms across her chest. "It's no coincidence you're here, is it?"

"I may have elaborated slightly to speak with you," I admitted. "Though I'd appreciate it if you'd finish the haircut."

Iris pursed her lips but eventually picked up her scissors. "What do you want?"

"Honesty and answers would be appreciated."

"About Cora? I can't help you," Iris said briskly. "Since you're here, you know we worked together. Or rather, I worked for her. But I put that behind me. That's a young woman's game."

"Not for Cora," I said. "While she was at the Rusty Nail, she entertained gentleman friends."

Iris chuckled. "Cora was unique. She had a way about her that had men eating out of her hand. I'd have given my right eye for half her charisma. She made it look so easy."

"She seemed popular when I met her at the pub," I said. "You can imagine my shock when I discovered she was dead."

"You found the body?"

"My landlady did," I replied. "But I was staying at the pub the night Cora died."

"That can't have been pleasant," Iris said.

"Seeing a body never is. But I'm interested in learning everything I can about Cora's life and the reason she died."

"Any knowledge I have about Cora is out of date." Iris snipped vigorously at my hair, and I hoped she wasn't hacking a chunk out of the back in a fit of pique. "I got out of that business and went legit. Helped set up this place with two other girls who quit at the same time. We took classes and practised on each other."

"How was Cora as an employer?" I asked.

"She was stern but fair," Iris said, a note of caution entering her voice. "Strict, yes. But she worked just as hard as the rest of us. The pay was good, and she took no nonsense from the clients. If anyone stepped out of line, if there was violence or disrespect, they were gone. She refused their custom, no matter how much they offered. We all appreciated that."

"When was the last time you saw her?"

"Oh, it's been a while. Months, I'd say."

"She never asked you to rejoin the business?"

"Cora always knew when it was time for a girl to go," Iris said. "She didn't want us getting jaded or broken down. Not just physically, but up here." She tapped the side of her head.

"I understand why it would take its toll," I said.

Iris shrugged as she worked on the side of my hair. "Not all of us have your opportunities. We find work where we can."

"You'll hear no judgement from me."

The door opened, and a well-dressed chap in his forties stepped inside. The receptionist swiftly approached and ushered him out.

Iris glanced at me in the mirror. "This is a ladies' salon. You'd think they'd have worked that out by now."

"Some men don't have the sense they were born with." I was careful to keep still. I didn't want a slip of the scissors, but I slid my gaze to the side. The receptionist led the man away from the building, but instead of seeing him off, she turned him down a side alley. Perhaps Iris hadn't entirely rid herself of her old ways.

Another hairdresser hurried through from a back room. "Iris, the postman has just been. There's a letter for you from that new passport place. It could be good news!"

"Don't bother me now," Iris snapped. "I'm with a client."

The girl flinched and dashed off with the letter.

"You need a passport?" I asked.

"I'm not sure what I need. All the rules have changed since the war," Iris said. "I wasn't even certain I could get one, being unmarried and all. You have to jump through hoops now if you want to leave the country. It didn't used to be like that."

"Given everything we went through, security has tightened," I said. "Where are you planning to go?"

"I've made no plans. It's just a fancy, that's all."

A fancy to suddenly apply for a passport so she could leave the country? Was Iris yearning for a holiday in an exotic location, or was she fleeing from something? Something that might see her spending time in prison for committing a heinous crime.

"You didn't seem surprised when I told you Cora had died," I remarked.

"I already knew. Even though I've left that business behind, it's a tight-knit group. You keep your ear to the ground about who's doing what and where."

"When did you find out about Cora's death?" I asked.

"This morning. I can't recall who told me. Probably one of the girls. They love a good gossip. People are saying Cora died in her sleep. She must've been near sixty, so I wasn't surprised."

"It seemed that way when I saw the body," I said. "But there were elements that alarmed me."

"Elements? What are you talking about?"

"Evidence, if you like. Small things out of place that made me wonder if someone killed Cora."

Iris thumped down the scissors. "And you're here asking me questions because you think I did it?"

"I'm interested in anyone who was associated with Cora."

"My association with her ended when I left her business. Our paths don't cross."

"She never visited your salon? You never went to the Rusty Nail?"

"No, and no. Now, it's time for you to leave."

I peered in the mirror. "You've left one side of my hair unfinished."

"That's what you get for accusing me of murder." Iris stepped back.

I stared at my damp hair, one side cut short and close to my jaw, the other long and brushing my shoulder. Since the situation couldn't get much worse, I pressed on with my questions. "Where were you at the time of Cora's death? She died after midnight. If you have an alibi, I can eliminate you from any further enquiries."

"Enquiries? You don't give up, do you?" Iris shook her head. "Cora looked after me. Gave me a job when no one else would. I appreciated that. I was grateful. It wasn't work I'd have chosen, but it meant I had money and someone looking out for me. We parted on good terms. I've no reason to want Cora dead."

"Then you won't mind providing an alibi, will you?" I said. "It's a simple question."

"I should throw you out for being so insulting," Iris snapped.

"You can tell it to me, or you can tell it to the police," I said. "If I've worked out you and Cora were connected, they will too. Eventually."

"I don't want the police poking around here," Iris muttered.

"Then give me the information, and I'll put in a good word." Not that it would carry any weight with Detective Chief Inspector Taylor, but perhaps passing the details to Sergeant Matthers might keep the police from sniffing too closely around Iris's less than legitimate business.

"I was here! I'm often here late for clients who work irregular hours."

"The girls you look after work in the brothels—"

"Hush," she hissed. "I don't want my other clients overhearing. My daytime customers are respectable ladies."

"Cora died in the early hours of the morning," I said. "Do you stay open that late?"

"Sometimes. I was here. I often am." Iris grabbed her scissors and pointed them at the door. "I'm done answering your questions. Take your dog and get out."

I looked once more at my damp, lopsided hair and sighed. "Could you just snip this side?"

"Unless you want to find out just how sharp these scissors are, you'll go now."

I collected my handbag, removed the salon gown, and dashed out, Benji trotting at my side. Along with my new dramatic hairstyle, I now had a new suspect.

Maudie told me Iris visited Cora at the pub, yet Iris claimed not to have seen Cora in months. There was a reason Iris lied about that. Was that reason murder?

Chapter 9

By the time I'd returned to work, my hair was dry. Sadly, it was still uneven. I tucked the long strands behind one ear and brazened it out.

I marched into the office, up the stairs, and towards my desk with Benji. He cared not a jot about my appearance. I could be covered in dirt and leaves, and he'd still adore me.

My long-time nemesis and constant source of irritation in the office, Bob Flanders, took one look at me, did a double-take, almost dropping his pipe, and burst into a horrific, raspy laugh. "Whatever have you done to yourself?"

I hunted in my desk drawer for a pair of sharp scissors. "Since when have you taken an interest in ladies' fashion?"

He was still laughing as he slouched over to my desk. "You look... bizarre."

"It is well within my power to alter my hair, but that face of yours is far more difficult to adjust."

His laughter faded, and his customary scowl returned as he tugged on his crumpled suit trousers. "Women like a mature gent. I've heard people say wrinkles make a face more expressive."

"Did the anti-iron society give you that dreadful information?" I gripped the long strands of my hair and pulled them around so I could see them. It was too risky to attempt such an endeavour without a mirror. I glanced at Bob. And I didn't need an audience, hoping I'd make a blunder and chop off an ear. "I'll be back in a moment."

"Before you go." Bob placed a restraining hand on my arm. "We need to talk about Cora Bellamy."

I glared at his grubby fingers. "I've nothing I wish to say to you about her."

A growl from Benji made Bob remove his hand from my arm, but he remained so close I could smell the stale coffee on his breath.

"You know any serious journalism comes to me or one of the other chaps," Bob muttered, keeping a wary eye on Benji.

"And your point is?" I held the scissors in a manner I hoped looked threatening.

His gaze slid to the blades. "Cora died in your pub, but that doesn't give you priority over the story."

"Has a journalist been selected as the lead on this investigation?" I asked.

"It'll be me. I'm the best journalist on this newspaper."

"More like the one with the most elaborate stains on his tie. Is that egg and brown sauce I spy?"

Bob rubbed a hand absent-mindedly down his stained tie. "If it turns out Cora was murdered in her bed, that'll make front-page news. That means your name won't be on it."

"I shall write her obituary, though," I said.

Bob grunted. "I suppose you will. That's your job. Although I don't see you doing much of it lately. How long were you down in Kent with your fancy man?"

"I had an extended holiday, and a well-deserved one. Unlike some people around here, I don't always appear to be unwell on a Monday morning following a heavy weekend at the local pub."

"That's a lie! You take it back! I work twice as hard as you."

"Twice as hard at being an unpleasant chap who stands in a woman's way when she needs to get about her business." I waved the scissors at him. "Now, if you don't mind."

Bob sidled out of the way, glancing over his shoulder now and again and muttering to himself. Irritating fellow.

After dashing into the lavatory, I took a deep breath and hacked at my hair. It took a good five minutes to get the sides reasonably even, and it still didn't look tidy. I should have asked Ruby for help.

I set down the scissors and looked at the hair I'd cut off. I hadn't asked for Ruby's help with anything recently. When I'd returned from Kent, she'd been so unwell. Pale, feverish, jabbering away in nonsensical talk. Thanks to the sterling efforts of the doctors, they'd got her stable, but since then, she'd been stuck in bed, suffering relapses, so I hadn't liked to bother her. And in truth, I didn't want to.

I tutted to myself. I always knew that having children was a dreadful idea.

Once I'd returned to the office, I pulled out the work I'd done on the obituaries and carried on. I'd written five more before desiring a break and a strong cup of tea to keep me going. Before I left my desk to make my brew, since our wonderful tea lady was nowhere to be seen, I telephoned Camille Hartley.

Her meetings with Cora would have given her access to intriguing conversations, or she could have seen things that were untoward, giving me a clue as to who ended Cora's life.

Someone answered the telephone, but unfortunately, Camille wasn't available. I left my home and work telephone numbers, so she could reach me at her earliest convenience.

Death and filing consumed the rest of the day. With my pile of obituaries completed, I left work only an hour later than planned. Robert and his cronies had long since gone, no doubt ensconcing themselves in the local pub to bemoan the state of the world and the rise of women in their profession.

Rather than go home, I drove to the Rusty Nail. I wanted to see how Maudie fared, and I'd yet to decide her future as my landlady. If I couldn't trust her, then I shouldn't have her in charge of anything. But when I learned why she'd taken the money, I felt a measure of sympathy. As I knew all too well, having an elderly, ailing relative lurking in the back of one's mind strained one's reason and sensibilities.

I wouldn't decide just yet about Maudie until this investigation had played out. And part of me didn't wish to endure the exhausting process of recruiting someone new. That was a good thing about Maudie. She knew the Rusty Nail backwards and forwards. She was a big part of why the pub remained so popular. That and the excellent pie and mash.

The evening was surprisingly chilly as we hurried inside the pub. The regular patrons had already settled in, and most of the tables set for dining were full. I was tempted to stop for a meal, but I had promised Matthew and my mother a fish and chip supper, and so I couldn't dally for long.

There was a server behind the bar, and when I enquired as to Maudie's whereabouts, her face paled.

"She's out the back. You shouldn't disturb her, though."

"Why not?" I asked.

"There's a man with her."

"And why shouldn't they be disturbed?"

The woman's eyes widened. "It's best you don't get involved."

"I absolutely am involved. Where are they?"

"He won't like it."

"I couldn't give two hoots what this man likes or dislikes. Through the back, is it?"

She nodded, her hands gripping a dirty glass.

I marched through to the back rooms, and the second I approached a closed door, I heard a raised male voice. I pushed it open without knocking and discovered Maudie backed against the wall. A tall, broad-shouldered, thickset man with barely any neck and a face like a sullen bulldog was jabbing a finger in her face.

He whirled around at the sound of the door opening. "Get out of here. This isn't your business."

"You're mistaken, sir. This is very much my business in the literal sense of the word," I said. "Maudie, is there a problem?"

"Miss Vale! I didn't know you were coming by this evening." Maudie was visibly trembling as her gaze flicked to me.

"I wanted to see how things were getting on. Given your situation, I'm glad I stopped by. And you are...?" I addressed the question to the thuggish gent.

"You're involved with this place, then?" the man asked.

"How astute of you," I said. "Yes, my family owns this pub, among others, and we don't appreciate strangers causing our employees trouble."

"There's no trouble here." He took a step back from Maudie. "I just don't like it when people withhold information."

"Perhaps Maudie is withholding information because you're not being forthright," I replied. "You have yet to tell me your name."

A muscle ticked in his jaw, but he made no sound.

"This is Mr Gilbert Renwick," Maudie said quietly.

He wheeled on Maudie. "You never mind telling her who I am."

"Mr Renwick, if you continue to threaten a member of my staff, there will be consequences," I said.

Benji stepped forward, his hackles lifted and head lowered.

"I'm doing no such thing." Mr Renwick retreated, though his hands remained fisted at his sides. "It's only right I get frustrated when I don't get what I'm due."

"And what do you believe you are due?" I asked.

"He was asking about Cora." Maudie almost whispered the words.

My eyebrows shot up. "Were you acquainted with Miss Bellamy?"

Mr Renwick turned on Maudie. He raised his fist towards her, but before he landed a blow, Benji leapt into action. With a fierce growl, he launched himself at Mr Renwick, his teeth catching around the man's wrist and dragging him to the floor.

"Get this flea-bitten mutt off me!" Mr Renwick bellowed, flailing as Benji attempted to drag the enormous man across the floor.

"You raised your fist at Maudie, so don't act surprised Benji came to her defence," I said.

"I wasn't going to hit the stupid old crone! Just show her what she had in store if she kept blabbing. Now get this thing off me!"

"Will you behave if I call Benji off?" I asked.

"You make me sound like a naughty schoolboy," Mr Renwick said. "Stop him. I'm bleeding!"

"He'll do more than draw a little blood if you don't calm yourself, sir," I said.

"I'm not here to cause trouble," he said.

"Your words do not match your actions." My gaze ran over Mr Renwick. Although his manner was thuggish, he was well-dressed and smart. A tailored suit, glinting cuff links, and polished shoes. He had money. "Benji, release him."

Benji moved back, still growling, his hackles raised.

"That dog's not safe to be out in public," Mr Renwick muttered, examining the tear in his suit jacket. "I could get an infection."

"What you've received is a lesson in manners," I said. "If you threaten any member of my staff again, you'll get more than a nip from Benji."

Mr Renwick hauled himself off the floor and shook out the wrinkles in his suit. He bared his teeth and opened his mouth as if to issue further threats.

"Benji. Attack!"

Mr Renwick yelped and snatched a chair to shield himself. But he need not fear. Benji never attacked to kill. His training taught him that the word was a command to drive someone away. And it worked beautifully.

Mr Renwick stumbled about for a few seconds before locating the door and figuring out how the handle worked. He shot into the corridor, Benji behind him, and several yelps of surprise erupted from the bar as the two burst through.

I followed, pleased to see Mr Renwick vanish through the pub's main door. Benji stood by it, tail wagging, then turned and trotted back to me. I returned to the private room to find Maudie slumped in a chair, still shaking.

"Whatever was going on?" I joined her.

She reached out, patting Benji gently. "Thank you for helping. I'm not sure what I'd have done if you hadn't shown up."

"Do you know that man?" I asked.

"Everyone knows Gil Renwick," she said. "He fancies himself the local gangster and runs a shady black-market enterprise. He made his fortune selling illicit goods during the war. Now that's over, he's turned his attention to other illegal activities."

"He was asking about Cora. Did you ever see them together?" I asked.

"No, but I'm not surprised they knew each other. Word is, he's getting into brothels too."

"I doubt he was seeking business advice from Cora," I said. "What did he want?"

"Gil wanted to know about her things," Maudie replied. "I told him the police took her belongings, but he wasn't pleased and said she must've kept something hidden away. Asked if we had a safe and wanted to see inside it."

"The nerve of the man! I wonder what Cora had in her possession that piqued his interest so."

"I couldn't tell you," Maudie said. "All I know is, I'm grateful you came when you did. He'd have used his hands on me."

"Indeed. He struck me as the sort of fellow who lacks any sense of decency."

Maudie smoothed her hands down her dress. "I should get back to work. It's busy tonight. They all want to know what happened to Cora."

"Keep your ears open for any gossip," I said. "I'm interested in what happened as well. But take ten minutes to compose yourself. We can't have you spilling drinks with shaking hands, can we?"

Her smile was wobbly. She took a deep breath. "Thank you. For everything."

I patted her shoulder then headed out of the pub with Benji. After all that excitement and finding a new name to add to the suspect list, we deserved a reward.

I purchased three fish and chip suppers with extra scraps for Benji and Felix, and we made our way home.

I'd just stepped through the door when the telephone rang. I picked it up, passing the wrapped parcels of food to Matthew, who'd ambled out of the kitchen, a smile spreading across his face as he saw what I'd brought.

"Veronica, is that you?" It was Camille Hartley on the other end of the telephone line.

"It is! Perfect timing. I've just returned home," I said. "I take it you received my message?"

"Yes. About that. I'm not sure how I can help." There was a note of caution in Camille's voice.

"You interviewed Cora shortly before she died. I'd be interested in seeing your work."

"Why? We were discussing her favourite dresses and visits to local fashion houses."

"Are you certain that's all you talked about?" I asked. "I don't believe Cora's death was an accident."

Camille was silent for several seconds. "Let's meet tomorrow. How about one o'clock at Sullivan's? It's the new tearoom on Broad Street, close to your office. Do you know it?"

"I've heard of it. I'll meet you there."

"Very well. I'd... I'd appreciate talking things through with a fellow professional."

I longed to ask more, but my mother was hollering from her bedroom that I needed to eat before the fish grew cold. "I shall look forward to it. Good evening, Camille."

We said our goodbyes, and I set down the telephone. My stomach growled, but I was far more intrigued by what secrets Camille might reveal than filling my stomach.

But first, it was time for a delicious tea, time with my beloved family, and adorable kittens. The adventuring would have to wait.

Chapter 10

I arrived at Sullivan's tearoom ten minutes early, giving me time to determine whether Benji would be welcome inside, which he was, and to browse the menu at my leisure without a waitress hovering and pushing for a decision.

The offerings sounded delicious. I was tempted by the ploughman's lunch, followed by a slice of the delicious Victoria sponge, if I had room. Which I felt sure I would. There was always room for cake.

Camille breezed in precisely on time, gave me a wave, and threaded her way around the tables to join me at a discreet corner table, where we could talk freely.

"Isn't this place charming?" She settled into her seat. "It's my first time here, but everyone says it's delightful. The bunting is adorable."

"The menu does sound appetising," I said.

"Good. I'm famished. I managed only a small piece of toast and a slurp of tea before I dashed out the door this morning." Camille studied the menu intently. "I like your new hair. It's not a style I've seen before."

I touched the side that I'd snipped at. "I'm experimenting with a new look. I went to a salon in Soho."

"Oh! I didn't take you for a Soho girl," Camille said.

"Sometimes it's good to try new things."

The waitress came and took our order. We both decided on the ploughman's platters and a pot of English breakfast tea between us.

Camille waited until the waitress was out of earshot before leaning closer. "We're well-versed in the serious side of life, aren't we?"

"I've found myself embroiled in a case or two that's taken me into some less-than-desirable situations," I said. "Life isn't without its trials."

Camille drew in a breath. "I wasn't sure I should talk to you, but I believe you can be trusted. And this is strictly off the record. What I'm about to share isn't about breaking a story or getting our names on the front pages. I know that's what we desire, but I don't believe this is the way to go about it."

"I'm fine with things being off the record," I said. "Does this have to do with Cora?"

Camille glanced about before nodding. "The night I saw you at the Rusty Nail was the third time I'd interviewed Cora. On each occasion, the company she kept alarmed me."

"Her gentleman friends, you mean?"

Camille raised her eyebrows, nodding knowingly. "Yes. Her friends, such as they were. Cora even invited me to what she referred to as an after-party when we'd finished late. I declined."

"Gracious. She wanted you to entertain her male friends?"

"I believe so. And the more I got to know Cora and her circumstances, the more worried I became that my story was untrue. Well, not untrue, exactly. Cora adored fashion. I do too, which is how we met. We were at a show, admiring the same dress. But I wondered how she came by the money to afford such finery."

We paused as the waitress returned with our tea and luncheon, then we resumed our conversation.

"Are you aware of Cora's past?" I asked.

Camille sorted through her ploughman's before heaping her fork. "I'd heard rumours about what she used to do, but I assumed it was from decades ago. After all, Cora was no spring chicken. Yet every time we met, men were fawning over her, buying her drinks, bragging about the gifts they'd given her. It was so blatant. I'm not one to be easily shocked, but I found it unsettling."

"I've only recently learned about Cora's profession," I said. "When she booked into the Rusty Nail, she presented herself as a genteel lady in search of a quiet place to relax. It was only after pressing my landlady that I discovered the truth. It's likely Cora still plied the trade she alleged to have abandoned in Belgravia."

"I'm glad we can discuss this so openly," Camille said. "I wasn't sure who I could speak to. I knew if I mentioned it at work, they'd insist we turn it into a story. But it's not respectable, and it's not something I wish to be associated with. I'm even considering scuppering the entire fashion show angle."

"I see no harm in publishing your story," I said. "Cora was always well dressed. People can remember her for her love of beautiful things, not just her tragic passing."

"Perhaps you're right. She won't want to be remembered for being a madam." Camille took a bite of buttered bread, cheddar cheese, and pickle. "But I'm still in two minds about what to do."

"About what in particular?"

"Publishing a story about someone so scandalous," Camille said. "I don't want to be seen as one of those dreadful gossip column types. Cora's associations were extensive, and the gentlemen who frequented her Belgravia club were well known."

"Would you mind sharing those names?" I slipped a small chunk of Cheddar cheese to Benji, who waited patiently beneath the table.

"I don't know exact names, but Cora's connections thread through influential halls of power. Men of interest, men of industry, politicians. I even heard a rumour that a minor royal indulged in her services."

"The men who visited her at the Rusty Nail clearly had money, but royalty? That seems a stretch."

"That's what the whispers told me," Camille replied. "With a list of names like that, Cora would have held considerable power."

"And if she ever made use of that power, she'd find herself in trouble." I set down my fork. That was quite a motive.

"I'd also wondered if Cora was still working," Camille said. "Why else would those men be hanging about?"

"A high-society madam is a well-paid occupation, but not one many women can sustain."

"That's what had me confused," Camille said. "Cora was a beautiful older woman, but would she still be entertaining clients at her age?"

"It does seem dreadfully exhausting," I said. "All that preening. She must have spent hours in front of the mirror."

Camille took a sip of her tea. "I'm barely managing as it is, running a small household and maintaining a full-time career. I couldn't handle the demands of multiple men as well."

I smiled wryly. "It must require extensive organisation and a great deal of careful juggling. Perhaps Cora had assumed more of a managerial role. She could have arranged younger girls to meet the men's... preferences."

"That makes sense. Although on one occasion, when I was leaving after an interview, Cora took a gentleman to her room. She was brazen about it. It was rather embarrassing to witness. Not that I think there's anything wrong with older women enjoying themselves in the bedroom, but if Cora was continuing those activities, I'm uncertain I want to write anything about her."

"I see your quandary. But breaking such a secret could make your career." I studied Camille closely. We were both career-focussed. Driven to make a name for ourselves. I found it hard to believe Camille would turn down such a cracking opportunity, exposing a woman who'd fashioned herself as a refined tastemaker, only to reveal she still practised one of the oldest professions known to women.

After the waitress had freshened our pot of tea, I pressed Camille further on the matter.

"Don't you get bored with writing fashion pieces?" I asked. "I enjoy the obituaries well enough, especially when the manner of death is unusual or the subject had a colourful life, but there are so many ordinary deaths, they scarcely warrant mention. I do my best for the deceased, but it can be a struggle."

"Everyone reads the obituaries, though, don't they?" Camille said. "There's a morbid fascination in learning who's died and how. I always enjoy yours."

"Thank you. I do my utmost to ensure a fitting and respectful send-off. But a story such as the one you're sitting on would be extraordinary."

Camille looked out the window. "When I first met Cora and realised there was more to her than she'd let on, I drafted an article about her deception. The women who attend the fashion shows are well-to-do, and they mingle in the highest of society circles. It would cause a stir if they learned a woman they often sat beside entertained gentlemen for money to fund her extravagant wardrobe."

I nodded slowly as Camille spoke. She'd written an expose on Cora. Perhaps Cora had discovered the truth, and they fought. But if they'd argued, there'd have been signs of a struggle. Bruises on Cora's body, possibly items damaged in the bedroom. There'd been none of that. Cora looked as though she'd simply fallen asleep and never woken.

"You were at the Rusty Nail the night Cora died," I said. "Was there anyone in her party who made you feel uncomfortable or gave you cause for concern?"

Camille furrowed her brow, deep in thought. "The men with her were a noisy bunch, but aside from a few inappropriate comments, they seemed respectful. I didn't feel unsafe around them. I didn't recognise any of their faces, but I suspect they were from the financial district. They all had that look, didn't they? Wearing the same style of tie, hair slicked back in the fashionable style. One of them mentioned working in the banking industry."

"What time did you leave Cora that night?"

"It was late. I'd started the interview, but then Cora needed to make some telephone calls, and I didn't care to remain in the men's company, so I ordered a late supper and sat in the nook, working on my story. Cora returned, and we spoke for another two hours, give or take. We might have finished sooner, but the men kept interrupting and attempting to be amusing. It was rather tiresome. The drunker they got, the less entertaining they were."

"You must have left the pub near closing time," I said. "I don't recall seeing you go."

"I left around half past ten that night," Camille said. "I didn't realise you were still at the pub, or I'd have joined you for a nightcap."

"I stayed the night," I said. "My landlady complained about Cora's company, and I wanted to ensure there was no funny business. That was why I was there when Cora's body was found."

"Oh, that makes sense. How shocking for both of you!"

"Indeed. Do you live nearby?" I asked.

"Not terribly. I can't afford the rent around here. Not on my wages. It's about an hour on foot, but I was fortunate enough to catch the last bus home. I was in bed just before midnight. Why do you ask?"

"To be frank, Camille, you were one of the last people to see Cora alive," I said. "I wouldn't be surprised if the police want to speak with you."

"Oh, what an inconvenience," Camille said. "I won't be of any use to them. I didn't catch any of the gentlemen's names and couldn't tell you where they worked."

"If they had any sense, they wouldn't have given you a real name," I said. "How about Cora? Did you part on good terms?"

Camille tilted her head slightly, her expression sharpening. "I know where you're going with this, but please don't. You have a keen mind and a vested interest in the case, but I didn't want Cora dead. I was writing about her. I needed her alive to finish the story."

"Do you have someone who can vouch for your arrival home?"

"You jolly well know I have no one special at home. I'm far too busy for all of that. I live alone, which means I've no definitive alibi, but I can assure you I don't need one. Cora gave me no reason to harm her."

I picked up my cup. "I had to ask. I want to get to the bottom of this mystery."

"Then perhaps I can assist," Camille said after taking a steadying breath. "As I left the pub, a woman stopped me and asked after Cora. She wanted to know if Cora was alone, and she wasn't pleased when I told her she had company."

"What did this woman look like?" I asked.

"She was short and shapely, with dark hair. Perhaps thirty years of age. And heavily made up. She smelled faintly of hairspray."

"Did she give you a name?"

"No, and I didn't ask," Camille replied. "I was tired. My eyes stung from the smoke in the pub, and I wanted to get home. She was well-dressed, though, in a style similar to Cora. Given everything we've learned, perhaps she was one of Cora's girls."

I sat back in my seat. Despite the risk to my hair and possibly my life, I needed to speak to Iris Dane again.

Chapter 11

"I've had Bob complaining about you." Uncle Harry leant back in his seat and regarded me levelly. "Have you been provoking the poor fellow again?"

"The provocation is necessitated by his irritating manner and his determination to make me quit this job," I replied tartly. "And you know full well I'll never do that."

I was settled opposite Uncle Harry, following my fascinating luncheon with Camille. I'd updated him on the situation with Cora and the Rusty Nail. Although Uncle Harry had no say in the pub's business affairs, he took a keen interest, especially when there was a murder involved to give him a front-page story.

Uncle Harry sighed. "I keep hoping he'll soften."

"Bob is of a different generation," I replied. "The men were in charge. Some of the younger chaps are open-minded enough to see the benefits of having women working, but alas, he's not one of them. I'm content to wait him out. The way he eats those fried egg sandwiches guarantees his heart can't last for much longer. I'll soon be writing a suitable obituary notice about him, though I don't expect he'll pay us to do it."

"Veronica! That's a terrible thing to say." Uncle Harry smiled broadly. "I'll give him a few lines even if he doesn't pay up. Now, I wanted to talk to you about another matter."

"A new story? Let me guess. Is it a church fete or a cake-baking contest you wish me to attend?"

"It's an ongoing story, and not one we'll write about," Uncle Harry said. "I've been speaking to your mother's new gentleman friend, Colonel Basil."

"Have you now? What reason did you have to speak with him?"

"It was Colonel Basil who reached out to me," Uncle Harry said. "He wanted a quiet word, man to man."

"That sounds serious. Is something amiss?" Colonel Basil became acquainted with us on our recent holiday to Margate and had continued a friendship with my mother.

"Hopefully, it's nothing amiss, but I wanted to keep you informed. Colonel Basil is very serious about Edith, so much so that he's considering a proposal."

I almost fell off my seat in surprise. "Good gracious! At their age?"

"I didn't realise love had an expiry date." Uncle Harry chuckled, but there was a sharp ring to it. His wife, my Aunt Sophie, had walked out on him, taking their two children, leaving him alone and heartbroken.

"I understand they've formed a friendship, but Mother has always said her heart belongs to one man," I replied.

"Which is why I want you to keep an eye on things," Uncle Harry said. "Colonel Basil seems like a fine gent, but I'm concerned this will be too much of a strain for Edith. We know how she can be with her nerves."

"I can imagine how she'd receive such a proposal," I said. "We'd have to send her to a country hospital for months because of her heart palpitations. I appreciate the warning. I shall advise Colonel Basil to look elsewhere if he's seeking a romantic relationship."

"That's just the thing. I'm not sure he is," Uncle Harry said. "He talked about friendship and being fond of Edith, but he didn't talk about romance as such. Still, we men don't. I assumed it was implied."

"Matthew will have a thing or two to say about this," I said. "He's not keen on Colonel Basil. The last time he spoke about him, he was worried the colonel was after our assets."

"The man doesn't seem short of a bob or two, so I'm sure that's not the reason for his interest in Edith. And didn't they bump into each other on that holiday down in Margate? He couldn't have conspired that."

I nodded. "Matthew is being protective, that's all."

"It's good he is. And he's doing much better, don't you think?" Uncle Harry said.

"Yes, the whole family is getting along splendidly," I replied. "Therefore, we want no bumps in the road, turning things upside down. The next time Colonel Basil reaches out to you, send him my way."

Uncle Harry's chuckle was louder this time. "I'm not sure I'd want to be in that poor chap's shoes when you give him a piece of your mind."

"It'll be a gentle piece," I said. "I just want to make sure he knows where he stands. Before I forget, I wanted to tap into your insider knowledge about a local criminal named Gilbert Renwick. Have we ever reported on his criminal activities?"

Uncle Harry's expression darkened. "Why do you want to know about a troublemaker like Gil?"

"He accosted Maudie in the Rusty Nail and asked questions about Cora. Benji saw him off," I said.

"You're fortunate to have come out of that encounter unscathed. Stay away from Gil Renwick. He's spiteful and mean."

"You've met?"

"No, and I don't want to meet him, but he's behind various criminal activities, and he's quick to wipe out the competition." Uncle Harry sat forward. "Veronica, I know you're fearless, but fear this man. Keep clear of him. If he had anything to do with Cora's death, let the police know, and then step away."

There was a knock on the door, and our wonderful tea lady, Doris, poked her head in. "Sorry to disturb you, but your telephone was ringing, Miss Vale, and no one was picking it up."

"How typical," I said.

"I thought it could be important, so I answered. There's a posh-sounding lady who demands to speak to you this very instant," Doris said.

"Thank you. I'll be right out." I nodded to Uncle Harry and left his office. The telephone was waiting for me on my desk. After spearing my lazy male colleagues with a glare, I picked it up. "Good afternoon, this is the London Times. Veronica Vale speaking."

"Yes, I know who it is, since I made the telephone call." Lady M sounded arch.

"Oh! Is something wrong with Ruby?"

"Very much so. She's bored and sick, and you are doing a most dreadful job of being her best friend."

I pressed my lips together. "Given the circumstances, I could say Ruby is fortunate I'm attending to her needs at all."

"The circumstances are that she's a young lady with difficult choices to make."

"Difficult choices she excluded me from," I said.

"I'm not one to flimflam with my words, so listen carefully," Lady M said. "You're a stubborn young thing. You have a brilliant mind and a determination you rarely see in a woman, perhaps apart from me, but that makes you intimidating to some."

"Not to Ruby! We've been friends forever."

"When one finds oneself in a new and uncertain situation, it leads to unwise decisions."

"At least we agree that what Ruby did was unwise."

"Don't be smug or act the fool," Lady M said. "You have a responsibility to your friend."

"I'm doing my best," I said through gritted teeth. "Work keeps me busy, and I'm investigating a murder. I have little time for myself, let alone to visit your estate to ensure Ruby isn't overtaxing herself."

"You can make excuses all you like, but you're avoiding the situation," Lady M retorted.

"I was at your house just the other day!"

"You stayed barely five minutes before finding a reason to leave."

"The doctor arrived! What was I supposed to do?"

"Wait outside and then return to ask how things were going," Lady M said. "Ruby was heartbroken you left so soon."

I inhaled deeply and exhaled slowly. "I promise I will visit later. And I shall bring her a treat. What would she like to eat? Is she able to keep food down?"

"She keeps complaining about feeling sick, but she has a fancy for anything sweet."

"Then sweet it is."

We said our goodbyes, and I set down the telephone. This was a situation I'd yet to resolve, and I couldn't keep making excuses. I had to make things right between Ruby and me, but I was at a loss about how to repair the damage to our friendship.

Rather than dwell on the sticky situation, I made a swift telephone call to the police station and requested to speak to Sergeant Matthers.

"I wondered when I'd hear from you," he said on the other end of the line. "I had an update from Sergeant Redcote about the goings-on at the Rusty Nail, and I thought, Miss Vale will want to know the latest."

"Please, Veronica is fine," I said. "Before we discuss the murder, how are you? Sergeant Redcote said you'd been injured."

"I appreciate you asking. I got whacked on the bonce by a drunk. He knocked me clean out."

"Oh, you poor thing. A blow to the head is never enjoyable."

"Well, from all the adventures you find yourself in, you would know better than most," Sergeant Matthers said. "But I'm back on duty and fit as a flea."

"Excellent news. I'm so glad you are. It was either talk to you or Detective Chief Inspector Taylor, and you know how close we are."

Sergeant Matthers laughed. "He's been cursing your name. He's half a mind to arrest you, since you were at the pub when the victim was found."

"I've no doubt he'd like to do that. You say victim?" I asked. "Does that mean you know the cause of death?"

"Yes, and it has me worried," Sergeant Matthers said, keeping his voice low. "Your pub was searched top to bottom, and any evidence taken away. We rushed through the tests and discovered that someone put strychnine in Cora's milk."

"Oh, my word. I noticed the half-drunk glass on the bedside cabinet," I said.

"There was a healthy dose of sugar added to the milk, which would have masked any bitterness," Sergeant Matthers said. "But this is what's got me worried. Am I right in thinking your landlady delivered a supper tray to Cora on the night of her death?"

"She did, but that wasn't unusual. Cora requested the same supper every evening."

"Can you confirm who was in the pub with you that night?"

"It was the three of us. Cora was in her room. I had a guest room, and Maudie was in her private lodgings, which are downstairs near the kitchen."

"Was there any way for someone else to gain access to the pub?"

"Maudie is careful about securing the doors, but the back door lock is feeble. There was also a window open in Cora's bedroom. For a healthy person, it wouldn't have been a treacherous drop if they were careful with the landing. And I noticed dirt on the ledge. It could have come from a boot."

"That's a possibility, but it's not one Detective Chief Inspector Taylor is interested in," Sergeant Matthers said. "We're to speak to your landlady again, and this time, it'll be a formal questioning. She's the most obvious suspect. It would have been a simple matter for her to put the poison into the milk before delivering it to Cora's room."

"Maudie would never do such a thing," I said sharply. "And you said yourself that you searched the pub top to bottom. Did you find any strychnine stashed away?"

"No, but Maudie could have disposed of it before we arrived. And it's a common enough poison used around here to deal with the rats," Sergeant Matthers said. "I'm sorry, Veronica, but we must do this."

I sighed. "When are you intending to speak to her again?"

"Officers are on their way to the Rusty Nail, and they'll bring her to the local station for questioning."

"I must be there too," I said. "Does Maudie know you're coming?"

"We telephoned her to let her know. Although I think she already knew we considered her a suspect."

"This is unacceptable," I said. "Make sure they don't take Maudie away until I arrive. I plan to be her representative."

"Which is why I'm telling you all of this," Sergeant Matthers said.

I released a pent-up breath. "Thank you, Sergeant."

"You can rely on me and Sergeant Redcote. We want the right outcome in the cases we investigate, yet we sometimes find, when our Detective Chief Inspector is involved, things go awry."

"That comes as no surprise. If I leave now, I can be at the Rusty Nail within half an hour," I said.

I dashed back to Uncle Harry's office, explained the situation, and then raced off with Benji, breaking numerous speed limits to ensure I got to the Rusty Nail as soon as possible.

I burst through the front door and discovered Maudie standing by the bar with a tall, thin man I recognised as Father Kersey, their heads bent close together as if in prayer. I stood back for a few seconds until they finished.

Maudie looked over, and her eyes widened when she saw me. "Veronica! I didn't know you were coming by."

I hurried over. "I just heard the news from the police. I'm here to support you. I won't let them take you in on your own."

She visibly sagged with relief. "Thank you. I didn't know what to do with myself. If Father Kersey hadn't been here..."

"But I am here, my dear lady," Father Kersey intoned. His voice had a deep timbre, perfect for lulling parishioners to sleep from his pulpit. "This is a test sent to try you. But you are a God-fearing woman, and you stand on the side of righteousness."

I grimaced. He was one of those priests who insisted every trial was divinely sent, and one had to endure it nobly. Sometimes, though, the trials were recklessly awful and heartbreaking, and I could find no divine reason for anyone to bear them.

"Pardon my manners. I don't think I introduced you." Maudie swiftly made the introductions.

I nodded politely to Father Kersey. "I recognise you. Do you often visit the Rusty Nail?"

"It's where many of my parishioners come, and I like to spend time with them. God sent me today to support my flock," Father Kersey said.

"I'm innocent," Maudie said to me, her voice trembling. "I'm in shock that the police think I had anything to do with it."

"Have they told you what evidence they found?" I asked.

"They think someone tampered with Cora's food, although they wouldn't say how."

"I understand Cora came from a troubled background," Father Kersey said. "I was wondering if perhaps she did this to herself." He made the sign of the cross, touching his forehead first.

"Cora didn't seem like a woman who'd give up the fight," I said. "And surely, if she'd poisoned herself, there would have been evidence in her room."

"Poison?" Maudie looked at me. "The police didn't say it was poison. Oh, this is dreadful."

"It's an uncomfortable situation, but I'll get you out of it," I said.

The pub door opened, and two police officers appeared, striding towards us.

Father Kersey touched Maudie's arm. "You will be in my prayers. I always make time in the evening to pray for the fallen."

I glowered at him. "I assure you, sir, no one here has fallen."

He mumbled a prayer and crossed himself again before scurrying off.

After the police escorted us to the station, we had to wait for half an hour before an interview room became free. All that time, Maudie sat in a seat, shaking and apologising to me.

I did my best to calm her, though I was angry with her and the police for being such fools. Maudie had been in the wrong for associating with Cora, so it was no surprise she'd come to the police's attention.

"What should I tell the police?" Maudie looked up at me as I paced, with Benji beside me.

"The absolute truth," I said. "You got yourself into a muddle, but as you told me, by killing Cora, you would have removed a vital source of funds. The police will look into the matter and see you're telling the truth."

As I spoke, her bottom lip trembled. "They think I did it."

"They're incorrect, but when looking only at the surface level, it's a reasonable enough assumption," I said. "Stick to the facts and try not to get emotional. Ah, here comes Sergeant Matthers. He's a sensible type, so he'll make sure you're treated fairly."

"Right this way, ladies. Sorry for the delay. It's been a busy day." Sergeant Matthers smiled warmly at me. "I don't know what's got into people these days. Too much drink and not enough sense, most likely, since our cells are full."

"Which is a relief for Maudie," I said, as we followed him into a small interview room that smelled of stale coffee. "It means you've nowhere to put her."

"They won't hold me, will they?" Maudie grabbed the back of a chair.

"They've no reason to," I said. "Once you've explained everything, we'll get back to the Rusty Nail, and this nasty business will be over."

Sergeant Matthers gave me a cautionary look and shook his head as we took our seats.

I didn't like that look. It suggested things wouldn't go our way.

"I'll get the formalities out of the way before we start the questions," Sergeant Matthers said. He noted Maudie's full name, age, and her address, which was a simple enough business. When he was done, he leant back in his seat and looked towards the door. "Sorry about this."

"Who are we waiting for?" I asked.

"Well, that's why I'm sorry," Sergeant Matthers said. "Detective Chief Inspector Taylor has taken an interest in this case. You didn't hear this from me, but he's got his appraisal coming up and wants to make sure he gets a win on the books."

"Oh, for heaven's sake! If we have to deal with that buffoon, this will take forever," I said. "Can't we have a more sensible fellow to assist you?"

"*I'm* assisting him," Sergeant Matthers replied. "I'll keep him on the right track. He's not conducted an investigation for some time, so his technique will be rusty."

We had to wait another five minutes before Detective Chief Inspector Taylor deigned to grace us with his presence. He strolled in, not seeming to realise or perhaps not caring how disgracefully late he was, and took a seat next to Sergeant Matthers.

"Let's get down to business, shall we?" He clapped his hands together and looked at us. His gaze narrowed a fraction as it lingered on me.

"Before you protest, I'm here in an official capacity," I said. "Maudie needs representation."

"You're a lawyer now, as well as a writer? And what do you like to call yourself? A private investigator, too?" Detective Chief Inspector Taylor smirked.

"It's surprising how many skills women can master when given the freedom to do so," I said.

He grunted. "I should be glad you're here, Miss Vale, since it was you or Maudie who committed this murder."

Maudie gasped.

"It was neither of us," I said. "But I'm glad we've spared you time by being here."

"There were only three women in that pub on the night Cora Bellamy was poisoned, and she didn't do this to herself. The logical conclusion is simple. Did you work alone or together?" Detective Chief Inspector Taylor asked with an air of smug satisfaction that made me want to slap him.

"The pub has windows and doors," I said. "Have you inspected them to see if anyone broke in?"

"My men always do a thorough job. They're trained professionals. Unlike some of us here," Detective Chief Inspector Taylor said.

"You shouldn't put yourself down. There are so many others happy to do it for you," I replied.

"There's no need to be tart with me. You're an untrained amateur." Detective Chief Inspector Taylor leant back. "You've had one or two successes, and that has given you an excess of confidence. But you've overstepped this time. Leave this matter to the professionals."

"Where might I find such professionals?" My hands fisted in my lap. The buffoon wanted me to lose my temper to give him an excuse to eject me from the interview, but I was determined to stay and assist Maudie.

"Veronica," Sergeant Matthers cautioned.

"I did not mean you, Sergeant Matthers." I shrugged a small apology.

"Talk us through the night Cora Bellamy died," Detective Chief Inspector Taylor said.

"Nothing has changed since I gave you my statement." Maudie glanced at me, and I nodded for her to continue.

"You permitted Cora to stay at the pub and conduct her... business?" Detective Chief Inspector Taylor asked.

"No! I didn't know what she was doing," Maudie said.

"That's not true. We've spoken to some gentlemen who used Cora's services, and after reassuring them their names would not be made public if they cooperated, they confirmed Cora used the Rusty Nail as a brothel."

"I would never permit such activities to take place in one of my establishments," I said.

"We have accounts from reliable chaps."

"Only after you threatened to ruin their social standing," I said. "That evidence won't stand up in court."

"We know what's been going on, so there's no need to get overexcited," Detective Chief Inspector Taylor said. "What I'm really interested in is how much you knew, Miss Vale. You consider yourself a clever woman, but is it feasible you missed what was going on right under your nose, or were you complicit?"

"I thought we were here so you could question Maudie, not me," I said. "And, as well you know, my father purchased dozens of pubs. I have skilled publicans looking after the day-to-day affairs. It would be impossible for me to know exactly what was going on at all times."

"If I may," Maudie said, "Miss Vale knew nothing about Cora. And I've admitted Cora gave me extra money to look the other way while she conducted her... affairs. That was all my doing. I knew it wasn't right, which was why I kept quiet. Then things got out of hand."

"How convenient that the cause of your troubles was poisoned," Detective Chief Inspector Taylor said. "I rather like the idea that you were in on it together. You attempted to oust Cora, but when she refused and threatened your esteemed reputation, you silenced her. I expect you hoped we'd think she died in her sleep, given her age. But I'm sharper than that."

"You're as sharp as a blunt spoon, if that's the direction you're going," I said.

"There's no need for spite," Detective Chief Inspector Taylor snapped. "We know poison was used to murder Cora. We also know Cora was pulling in a handsome sum of money for the privilege of using your rooms as a brothel."

I drew in a breath to steady my rising temper. "Maudie has accepted that what she did was wrong. She has a seriously ill sister who requires care. She's unable to work at the Rusty Nail and care for her, so she employs people to do it. That was the only reason she let Cora take advantage of her."

"Her poor, sick sister. Is that what she told you?" Detective Chief Inspector Taylor smirked again. "It really is fortunate there are experts managing this case. Maudie's sister has been dead for weeks."

"Sir, you are misinformed." I looked at Maudie, who'd shrunk in her seat. "Tell them it's untrue."

Maudie wouldn't look at me. Instead, she fixed her gaze on the wall. "I did need money to care for my sister. That part is true. The doctors couldn't figure out what was wrong with her, so the best I could do was get her care at home and make her comfortable. And then... then she died, and I needed money for the funeral. She told me what she wanted, and it wasn't cheap. But I needed to give her a good send-off."

I closed my eyes for a second, my stomach dropping. "So you kept taking Cora's money."

"And she'd have continued to do so, despite no longer needing the extra funds," Detective Chief Inspector Taylor said, a note of triumph in his voice. "Perhaps, Miss Vale, you're not as astute as you'd like to think you are. Allowing such indiscretions threatens your licence. I should make a telephone call to the licencing board and inform them of your scandalous behaviour."

I was so angry with Maudie, I could barely breathe. And having Detective Chief Inspector Taylor jabbing at me and threatening my livelihood made my anger rise to a high simmer.

Sergeant Matthers cleared his throat and shuffled in his seat, drawing my attention to him. He shook his head meaningfully.

"Whatever is the matter with you?" Detective Chief Inspector Taylor said to him.

"Sorry, sir." Sergeant Matthers kept his attention on me. "Too much starch in my collar."

"Pull yourself together. We need Maudie's confession and perhaps Miss Vale's too. That would be a fine end to the day, securing the convictions of two impertinent criminals."

"No one in this room is a criminal." I drew back my anger just enough to speak without sounding shrill. "Maudie made a mistake, perhaps more than one, and she will pay for that. But that mistake wasn't murder."

"Then explain this to me, my dear Miss Vale," Detective Chief Inspector Taylor said. "The three of you were locked in the Rusty Nail. And yes, I admit, there are doors and windows someone could have entered, but there was no sign of a break-in."

"There was an open window in Cora's bedroom," I said. "And her door lock needed fixing."

"No one would be fool enough to jump out of a window," Detective Chief Inspector Taylor said.

"A killer would," I said. "Someone fit and strong who needed a fast getaway."

"Preposterous! It was one of you. I wish I could pin this murder on you, Miss Vale, but I think it was Maudie. She had access to Cora's room, and she provided the poisoned milk."

"Maudie had no motive to commit murder. Cora was causing her embarrassment, yes, and she was worried the ruse would be discovered—"

"Exactly," Detective Chief Inspector Taylor interrupted. "She got in over her head and needed a way out."

"You have no witnesses. Yes, Maudie prepared the drink, but that doesn't mean she put poison in it," I said. "You have no solid evidence to show it was Maudie. If she'd grown used to having more money thanks to Cora's generosity, why would she kill her?"

"Because the money was no longer worth the inconvenience," Detective Chief Inspector Taylor said. "We're holding Maudie. An overnight stay in the cells may provide her with clarity of thought."

"You can't do that!" I said.

"I can do whatever I damn well like, and you won't stop me."

"I mean, keep on top of your own affairs. Sergeant Matthers told me you've no free cells. Maudie will return home, where she rightly belongs."

Detective Chief Inspector Taylor glowered at me for an uncomfortable amount of time. "Sergeant Matthers, find an empty cell for Maudie. Throw out some drunks if you need to. We can't risk her absconding before she makes a full confession."

Sergeant Matthers shot me an apologetic look before dashing from the room.

"Before you make this ridiculous and incorrect error, there's another suspect you must consider," I said.

"My men have questioned everyone of interest." Detective Chief Inspector Taylor pursed his lips, making him look like a bloated toad.

"What about Iris Dane? She worked for Cora at the Belgravia brothel. She's gone straight and runs a salon in Soho, but I fear she's conducting her old profession on the side."

"Why should that interest me? I stay out of Soho."

"Iris visited Cora at the Rusty Nail on the night she died." I glanced at Maudie. "That's significant."

"The only thing of significance is that we've captured our murderer." Detective Chief Inspector Taylor pushed back his chair.

"At least speak to Iris," I said. "I have a witness who will confirm Iris went to the pub."

Detective Chief Inspector Taylor hesitated. "The witness is reliable?"

"Reliable enough."

"It's of no matter. This information won't change my mind as to what happened at the Rusty Nail." Detective Chief Inspector Taylor rested his hands on the table. "Make this easy on yourself and confess."

Maudie drew in a shaky breath just as Sergeant Matthers returned.

"I've got a cell, sir."

"Excellent. Take the suspect away. A night alone with her thoughts will bring a change of mind by morning. I can guarantee it," Detective Chief Inspector Taylor said.

"I suppose you want to lock me up, too," I said.

"It's ever so tempting. You're nothing but an irritation and an obstruction whenever we have a murder to investigate," Detective Chief Inspector Taylor snapped. "But as you've smugly pointed out, we've little room for troublemakers. Your time will come."

"I know I've done you wrong." Maudie grasped my hand just before Sergeant Matthers led her out. "But I am innocent."

"We'll sort this out," I murmured before she was led away, sniffling.

Detective Chief Inspector Taylor rubbed his hands together. "Should I escort you off the premises?"

"I can see myself out."

"Keep out of mischief, or I will find you a cell."

I ignored him and wasted no time dashing to Soho. If the police wouldn't investigate the connection between Iris and Cora, I would. I needed to find the killer to ensure Maudie would go free.

It was late by the time I reached the salon. There were no lights on, but I detected a faint glimmer around the back. I dashed along the alley with Benji beside me.

It took me only a moment to find a door. It was ajar, so I pushed my head in and called out, "Hello? Is there anyone there?"

There was no reply, but the light was brighter back here, so I hurried along the passageway. The powerful scent of cigar smoke and alcohol suggested that the salon was just part of the business affairs taking place in this building.

"Iris? Are you there?" I called out louder. "It's Veronica Vale. You cut my hair recently. I must speak to you."

I pushed open the first door I came to and stopped dead. Iris was on her back, her sightless eyes staring at the ceiling.

Chapter 12

The shock of finding Iris dead slipped from me, and I rushed into action, dashing towards her.

I crouched near her shoulder and checked for signs of life. The large pool of blood beneath her and those vacant, unblinking eyes told me everything I needed to know.

Benji whined and nudged his nose against my leg.

"Yes, it's a terrible pity," I murmured, still staring down at the woman.

This wasn't an accident. There was a clear puncture wound and a tear in her dress from a blade.

By now, my eyes had adjusted to the low light. I stood, taking several minutes to assess the room. There was no sign that the murder weapon had been left behind, but several overturned pieces of furniture and a smashed glass indicated a struggle. Iris had not gone quietly. For that, I was glad. A vicious attacker deserved everything he got.

Benji's ears pricked. He turned to the door, his tail raised.

I was instantly at his side, knowing his hearing far surpassed mine. He took several steps forward and growled, hackles lifting. I settled a hand on his head to quiet him. It was easy to become nervous around a corpse, but that was not what bothered Benji.

I grabbed a fire iron from the small hearth and headed into the gloomy corridor. If I found a light switch, it would be too great a risk to use it. But if someone was in here, they must have heard me call Iris's name.

Her body was still warm, so she had died within the past half-hour. I may have even disturbed her killer, preventing their escape.

"Come out. I know you're hiding in here." I pushed as much command and strength into my voice as I could muster. "Give yourself up. There's nowhere to hide."

The building was sizeable, with many places for someone to secrete themselves, hoping not to be found.

"I've already telephoned the police. They'll be here in a matter of minutes." I would have called them had there been a telephone in the room where Iris lay.

Benji stayed still by my side, his ears up.

"I'll give you two minutes to show yourself." I slid open the door that led into the salon and dashed to the front desk, where I'd seen a telephone during my visit. I connected with the police, whispered the address and the situation before swiftly setting down the receiver.

The police could be inept, but I knew when to summon help, especially if there was a killer armed with a knife.

There was a thump some distance away, inside the building, suggesting whoever was hiding had bumped into a piece of furniture.

I crept back into the corridor with Benji. "We are armed, and we shall use our weapons if necessary." I kept walking and peered into the room where Iris lay then carried on along the corridor to explore more rooms. These were most likely used for Iris's other business.

Sure enough, one room contained a bed. Another smaller chamber held salon supplies and cleaning equipment.

I was backing out of the room when Benji barked sharply. A second later, I was roughly shoved into the cleaning cupboard, and the door slammed shut. Benji's barking grew frantic but fainter. He was pursuing my attacker!

I launched myself at the door, but it was locked or had been wedged shut and refused to budge. Benji was still barking. I heard a muttered curse and a warning.

Benji must have cornered the rapscallion!

I slammed my shoulder repeatedly against the door. I had to get out and help, but the wood was solid and refused to budge. I tugged at the handle, pulling one way and then the other. All the while, Benji's barking grew more frantic, though still some distance away.

After hunting among the supplies, I found a small toolbox containing a hand axe and a screwdriver. I attempted to unscrew the handle, but was unable to gain sufficient purchase. I then turned my efforts to the wood, focussing on the area around the handle to damage the lock. It took several minutes and some very unladylike cursing before the wood splintered.

I wedged the screwdriver between the door and locking mechanism, backed up as far as I could, then charged. I smashed out of the door with such force that I collided with the opposite wall, severely bruising my shoulder and arm. There was no time to concern myself with that. Benji was still barking, which meant he needed my help.

I oriented myself towards the sound and sped off, clutching my left shoulder. The dazzling pain suggested a dislocation.

There came another curse then a growl of warning from the man Benji had cornered.

And then Benji yelped, causing my heart to stutter. His barking abruptly stopped.

I took a sharp breath. Panic rose within me, terrible possibilities racing through my mind and lending my steps welcome speed.

Before I found Benji, a tall figure dressed in dark clothing with a hat pulled low over his face surged towards me.

I ran straight at him, and we collided in a tangle of limbs and curses, most of them coming from me. I attempted to yank the man's hat off, but he shoved me aside and slashed out with his right hand. His blade scored across my middle, tearing my clothing.

My hand flew to my stomach.

He grabbed me, turned me to face the wall, and slammed me into it, rattling my teeth. The jarring impact made me see stars. I was bracing to retaliate, but by the time I'd turned, he'd gone. A door slammed in the distance.

I drew in several shaky breaths then gently eased my hand from my stomach to assess the damage. Though the skin was pierced, it wasn't deep. There was blood on my hand, but nothing vital was slashed. I might need a stitch or two, but I would heal fully.

My gaze cut to the direction the man had fled, but I was in no fit state to pursue him. And I had to see to Benji, who was worryingly silent.

I ran along the corridor, and a gasp left my lips as I spotted him on his belly.

He wagged his tail weakly when he saw me. I dropped to my knees, my hands gently running over every inch of him in search of injury. There was no blood, so he'd not been stabbed. Benji attempted to rise, and that was when I saw the problem. It was his right paw. He couldn't put any weight on it.

"Oh, you poor fellow." I gently squeezed the paw to check for broken bones until his whimper made me stop. "You're so very brave, my darling. We'll find the cad who did this to you and Iris and make him pay. First, we must get you healed."

I scooped my undamaged arm beneath Benji's stomach so he wouldn't put weight on his damaged foot, and together we made our way slowly along the corridor, both of us whimpering and panting with effort and pain.

We made it partway along the corridor, but blackness seeped into my vision. I braced myself against the wall and slid as my body shut down.

Loud hammering at the front of the salon jerked me awake. Benji was pressed against me, never leaving my side no matter the trial.

I groaned as I eased myself back up, telling Benji to stay where he was, so as not to put undue pressure on his injury.

As I entered the salon, I grimaced. Sergeant Matthers and Sergeant Redcote were outside, but they weren't alone. Detective Chief Inspector Taylor was with them.

Damn and blast it. What was that lazy prig doing out? He scarcely left his office unless it was to visit the golf course.

It took me a few moments to figure out how to undo the lock, but it finally popped, and the policemen entered.

"Veronica, you're injured!" Sergeant Matthers gripped my shoulders to stop me swaying.

I winced. "If you wouldn't mind a gentler touch, Sergeant. I think I have a dislocation."

"What mess have you got yourself into this time, woman?" Detective Chief Inspector Taylor snapped as he marched in.

"I'm only in this mess because you refuse to do your job," I retorted, my pain making me forget all sense of decorum or manners. "This is where Iris works. Or rather, worked. She's dead in one of the private parlours she used to entertain gentlemen."

His gaze flicked to my injuries and the blood that had soaked through my clothing. "How serious is it, Sergeant?"

"If you don't mind my checking." Sergeant Matthers gestured at my stomach.

"Go ahead. The cut isn't deep. Iris's murderer was still on the premises when I arrived with Benji. The man slashed at me with a knife before fleeing. If you're quick, you might find him on the street. He's only been gone five minutes. Well, perhaps ten. I briefly lost consciousness." I checked my watch and frowned. I'd been unconscious for almost thirty minutes.

I was going to ask what took the police so long, but since Detective Chief Inspector Taylor was in attendance, I could guess the reason.

"I'll look outside." Sergeant Redcote dashed out the front and stood in the street, scanning in both directions.

"Where's the body?" Detective Chief Inspector Taylor glanced around the salon.

"As I said, she's in a back room." I hissed as Sergeant Matthers gently inspected my wound. "It's the first door you come to. It's open. Iris is on the floor, so you can't miss her." Although knowing his shortcomings, he could step over a body and not notice.

"Other than the shoulder, Veronica's injuries aren't severe." Sergeant Matthers straightened. "Would you like me to look at the body, sir?"

"No, I'll inspect the scene and see what we're dealing with," Detective Chief Inspector Taylor replied, as though it were a great inconvenience to do his job. He glared at me before striding away.

"Why did you have to bring him?" I whispered to Sergeant Matthers.

"He was there when your telephone call came in," he replied. "He's taken a particular dislike to you."

"I daresay he dislikes anyone who shows him up for the fool he is," I muttered.

"You need to rest," Sergeant Matthers said. "I see you're in pain."

"My shoulder is troubling me." I leant against the reception desk. "But what troubles me more is Iris. Her murder causes me a problem. I came here to confront her because I believed she killed Cora."

"She could still have done it," Sergeant Matthers said. "Perhaps Iris's murder is retaliation for what she did to Cora. Did you see who it was?"

"No. It was a man," I said. "Tall, wearing dark clothing and a hat pulled low. I could barely see his face, but he was strong, so I don't think he was old. He smelled odd. He was wearing a strange cologne. I can't quite place it, but I know that smell from somewhere."

"Once you've recovered from the shock of being stabbed and having your shoulder dislocated, your memory will be sharper." Sergeant Matthers raised his eyebrows. "You do find yourself in curious situations."

I half-smiled. "We can't have life getting dull now, can we?"

Detective Chief Inspector Taylor stamped back into the salon. "I don't know what ridiculous game you're playing, Miss Vale, but it stops now."

"I'm not playing any games. As you can see, I've been injured, as has my dog. We both require treatment."

Detective Chief Inspector Taylor's scowl deepened. "You've a nerve wasting our time like this. I'm arresting you."

"You're making no sense," I said. "Now, I'm aware I'm injured and not at full capacity, but why on earth would you arrest me? I didn't stab Iris."

"You're right there. No one did."

I stared at Detective Chief Inspector Taylor. "Then why is her bloodied body in the next room?"

"There is no body!"

Chapter 13

"You must have looked in the wrong room. Allow me to show you where it is." I slid past, ignoring Detective Chief Inspector Taylor's protests.

Benji sat in the corridor. He stood when I appeared.

"Stay where you are," I instructed, so he wouldn't put weight on his injured paw. I entered the room to show Detective Chief Inspector Taylor Iris's body.

It wasn't there. The rug she'd been sprawled on was also gone, leaving no trace of blood on the floor.

"What the devil is going on?" I murmured.

"Explain yourself, Miss Vale." Detective Chief Inspector Taylor spoke from behind me. "I assume I looked in the right place."

"Iris was right here!" I jabbed a finger at the space where Iris had been. "And look around. There are signs of a struggle. Knocked-over furniture, a broken glass."

"All I'm concerned with is a body. You must have been hysterical when you contacted the police to report that a woman was dead."

"I am never hysterical," I said.

"Your actions speak otherwise," Detective Chief Inspector Taylor said. "In a desperate attempt for attention, you've made a complete fool of yourself."

"I leave the foolishness to you, and I would never desire your attention," I replied. "You know what this means, don't you?"

"That I'm arresting you for wasting police time? Believe me, it's long overdue."

"Iris's killer has an accomplice! Perhaps the accomplice was at the Rusty Nail on the night Cora was murdered. They worked together to ensure they could get in and out of the pub undetected."

"Enough! Idle speculation gets us nowhere."

I frowned as I considered the possibility. "Although the methods of murder are entirely different. That's odd. Maybe the killer came here to warn Iris off, but she reacted violently, so he stabbed her."

Sergeant Matthers stood in the doorway. "There'll be an explanation. Perhaps there was an accomplice, sir. It's tricky to get one over on Veronica, so she could be on to something."

"I am quite done with her nonsense," Detective Chief Inspector Taylor said. "Arrest her. She's spending a night in the cells. Miss Vale, you have wasted valuable police time, and that's an offence. It's time you learned a lesson. You've no authority over my men. You're not a qualified detective, capable of solving complex cases."

"I could list many cases I've solved that would have had your head spinning on that puny neck," I said.

"Luck doesn't make an expert," Detective Chief Inspector Taylor said. "You've embarrassed me one too many times. This will be your lesson. Sergeant, handcuff Miss Vale and take her to the cells."

"Why would I lie about there being a body?" I protested.

"For attention. Because you're having a hysterical episode. Because you delight in trying my patience," Detective Chief Inspector Taylor snapped.

"All I want is to understand what happened to Cora and to ensure Maudie isn't charged for a crime she did not commit." I noticed Sergeant Matthers edging reluctantly towards me.

If Detective Chief Inspector Taylor persisted in this ridiculous notion, Sergeant Matthers would have no choice but to put the handcuffs on me. Although I hoped he wouldn't, given my troublesome shoulder. I liked Sergeant Matthers, and I knew he needed this job, so I wouldn't protest if it came to it.

I tried one last attempt to get this buffoon to see sense. "Detective Chief Inspector Taylor, use your extensive expertise. Analytically and dispassionately assess the situation. Look at the evidence before you. What is this room telling you?"

"It's telling me I should be enjoying a steak dinner with a local councilman at this very moment. Instead, I'm chasing after you and your wild fantasies."

I glowered at him. That was why he was so sour. He was missing a free evening of wining and dining, where a councilman would grease his palm to have a misdemeanour overlooked.

"Why don't you go to your steak dinner?" I said as sweetly as possible. "I'll sort everything out with

Sergeant Matthers. There's no need for you to worry about a thing."

"I won't worry about anything once you're behind bars," Detective Chief Inspector Taylor replied.

Hateful man. He was determined to see me locked away.

"Iris visited Cora the night she died," I persisted. "Perhaps she saw something she shouldn't and came to the attention of Cora's killer, who sought her out and silenced her. Perhaps he would have used poison again, but Iris discovered him before he could dose her drink and flew into a rage. She had a temper. She even terrified me."

"That's enough overtaxing of your little mind," Detective Chief Inspector Taylor said. "You're spending the night reflecting on what you've done. In the morning, you'll discover the full extent of the charges I shall bring against you. Sergeant, if I have to tell you again, you'll receive a formal warning. Put Miss Vale in handcuffs."

"There's no need for that," I said. "I'll come quietly."

"Then I won't have the satisfaction of seeing you bested." Detective Chief Inspector Taylor smirked. "The handcuffs. Now."

Sergeant Matthers made a show with the handcuffs, although he didn't tug on my injured arm and didn't secure them. He winked at me before leading me out.

I turned to Detective Chief Inspector Taylor. "To be clear, sir. You will never best me."

Three hours later, after having my injuries treated and being left alone with only my thoughts, I wondered whether Detective Chief Inspector Taylor might, after all, have got the better of me.

My single cot was smooth and cold, and my blanket was far from sturdy. I hadn't been allowed to keep Benji with me, but Sergeant Matthers promised to look after him, and I trusted the fellow to do right.

I was worried about Benji's injury. I'd slipped Sergeant Matthers money so he could take Benji to the vet. Benji would hate that, but I needed to ensure he hadn't come to serious harm while defending me.

A door at the far end of the corridor to the cells was unlocked, and footsteps approached. This had happened several times throughout the night, as other prisoners were released or moved. So, I was surprised when the steps stopped outside my door.

It was Sergeant Matthers. "You really do have luck on your side. You're free to go."

"Gracious! What splendid news. Detective Chief Inspector Taylor had a change of heart?" I stood and smoothed my crumpled clothing.

"That would be pushing your luck too far." Sergeant Matthers unlocked the cell door. "Your friends in high places heard about your dilemma."

"To whom are you referring, and how did they learn of my current situation?" I stepped through the doorway.

Sergeant Matthers grinned and tapped the side of his nose. "I can't say too much, but I needed to make sure Benji had somewhere to stay after his vet visit. And before you ask, he's fine. The vet cleaned up the injury and prescribed rest. He's on some pills, but he'll make a full recovery."

I kissed Sergeant Matthers' cheek. "Thank you for taking such excellent care of him. Benji will hate resting. He lives for his long daily walks."

"If he doesn't rest, he could permanently damage the leg."

"I'll make sure he behaves," I said. "But there's more to your story. Please go on."

"I'll tell you as we walk. Follow me. I've completed the paperwork, so you won't need to wait around."

"You are a dear man." I gently pressed his arm.

"I've always had a soft spot for you, especially after everything you did for Jacob." Sergeant Matthers cleared his throat. "Once Benji had been seen by the vet, I took him to stay with Lady M."

"Oh! That's resourceful of you," I said. "I assumed you'd take him to my mother's or the Rusty Nail."

Sergeant Matthers tugged awkwardly at his collar. "Well, here's the situation... Lady M asked me some time ago to keep an eye on you."

My mouth dropped open. "Sergeant! You're spying for Lady M?"

"No! Well, I wouldn't have put it quite like that. But she bought me a fine case of brandy and one of those fancy Harrods hampers. She said it was a thank you for keeping her informed of your... movements."

I swatted his arm, unsure whether to feel outraged or amused. The very nerve of that woman. "You absolute rotter! And you're a terrible spy, since you've just confessed everything."

"I felt ever so guilty about it," he admitted. "But I assumed there was a good reason Lady M wanted you watched. And I've noticed Ruby hasn't been about, even though I know you found her. I wondered if there was trouble between you two, and perhaps Lady M was the go-between."

"Ah! It's a little more complicated than that," I said carefully, being sure not to betray Ruby's confidence. That was her secret to keep.

Sergeant Matthers passed me my personal effects and some paperwork to prove I was a free woman. "I figured as much. Anyway, I decided I was overdue reporting back to Lady M, and I know she loves dogs, so I took Benji to her. While I was there, I mentioned your predicament."

"Well, even though you're a snoop, I appreciate the help," I said. "So does Benji."

I'd be in all sorts of trouble with Lady M, since I'd promised to visit Ruby. At least I had a solid excuse.

"There's more. When Lady M learnt of the situation, she made a few telephone calls and then insisted on coming to see you freed."

My eyebrows rose. "Lady M is in the building?"

"Naturally, I am. I had to ensure this nonsense was rectified." Lady M appeared from around the corner and strode towards me, her loyal chauffeur behind her. "Honestly, Veronica, what do you get yourself into?"

I failed to hide my surprise. "I'm solving a murder. Well, two."

"You do make life more interesting." Amusement glittered in Lady M's eyes. "I shall have the best gossip at my bridge club this week, all thanks to you."

"I'm happy to be of service," I said. "And thank you for ensuring Detective Chief Inspector Taylor saw reason."

"I had nothing to do with that tedious chap," she said. "I wished you to be free, and I made it so."

"It pays to have friends in positions of power," I murmured to Sergeant Matthers.

"Indeed, it does," Lady M answered for him. "Although your friends in not-so-high places do sterling work. Sergeant Matthers is a capable fellow."

He blushed. "Benji was happy when he went inside. I heard someone call his name—"

"Yes, I have a guest staying with me," Lady M said briskly. "Thank you, Sergeant Matthers. That will be all." She dismissed him as though he were one of her footmen, and he bowed slightly before backing away.

I hurried after Lady M and her chauffeur. Her large car waited just outside, parked shamelessly in the reserved area for police vehicles. The chauffeur opened the door for us, and we settled on the comfortable back seats.

"I assume the food was dreadful in that grim little place," Lady M remarked. "I'll have Cook prepare you a plate when we get home."

"We're going to your home? At this hour?"

"Where else? Or do you intend to let Ruby down again?"

"No! But I need to bathe and tell my mother and Matthew what's going on. They'll be beside themselves with worry."

"That has been seen to," Lady M replied. "Though you may use my telephone to reassure them when we arrive. I spoke to your charming brother. What a delight he is.

Very well-mannered and polite. I promised him I would take the very best care of you."

"I'd still like a moment to freshen up," I said. "Prison cells have a unique odour. And I was injured. I still have some blood on my skin, and this blouse will never recover."

Lady M wrinkled her nose. "I have plenty of fragrances and lotions. You may avail yourself of any you wish. But no more delays. Ruby misses you. She may not say as much, but she is lonely. I keep her company as much as I can, but I'm a busy woman, and we are of considerably different generations. She needs you, Veronica. No more excuses."

"Getting stabbed and arrested is hardly an excuse!"

Lady M speared me with a frosty glare, sniffed, then turned her gaze forward as we moved through the London streets.

There was no arguing with her, so I settled back into the seat. "How is Benji?"

"He had a steak dinner and fell asleep beside a roaring fire. The paw looks tender, but there's no infection. I personally gave him his first dose of medication, and he was such a good boy."

"He always is," I said fondly. "He was injured while helping me stop a killer."

"Goodness gracious! How shocking. You must tell me everything."

Thirty minutes later, we were at Lady M's sprawling estate, and she'd been informed of everything I'd endured while investigating Cora Bellamy's murder.

"This will absolutely delight Ruby," Lady M said with satisfaction.

"The fact I was stabbed and had my shoulder dislocated?"

"Foolish girl! I know she misses the thrill of the chase."

"Given her condition, she shouldn't be chasing anything. Not even a stray piece of paper caught in the breeze."

Lady M sighed, her joy fading. "Yes. Impending motherhood isn't doing her any good at all."

"If she's feeling unwell, I don't want to intrude."

Lady M grasped my hand. "You have ten minutes to freshen up. I'll have Cook plate you something, and then, it's time you and Ruby made peace. I shall not permit you to leave until you do so."

I longed for peace. Although I worried it would be simpler to solve this double murder than unpick the tangled, frayed remains of my friendship with Ruby.

Chapter 14

Despite the late hour, Ruby was settled on her usual chaise longue in the parlour Lady M had provided for her. She wore a voluminous nightgown, covered by a silken robe, and a full face of makeup. Despite the added colour, I could tell Ruby hadn't slept. Her cheekbones appeared sharper than usual, suggesting she was having trouble keeping food down.

Even though she was tired, she'd been transfixed as I'd retold my evening adventures, Benji's head wedged firmly on my lap to ensure I didn't leave him.

"It could only happen to Veronica." Lady M joined us in the parlour, followed by a server with finger sandwiches and tiny cakes.

"She always finds herself in elaborate situations," Ruby remarked. "I miss it. All the fun and danger."

"This will all be over soon. Do... do you have a plan?" I glanced at her ever-growing bump.

"Of course. You're not the only one who can make plans," Ruby said.

I waited, hoping she'd elaborate, but Ruby wasn't forthcoming.

"How did your mother respond to the news you'd been locked up like a hardened criminal?" Ruby asked.

"Thanks to Lady M and Matthew, she only suffered a few dozen palpitations," I replied.

"She's the one who raised such an adventurous spirit," Lady M observed. "She must be used to it by now."

"It was always my father who took me on adventures," I said. "He taught me to swim, to build a fire outdoors. He even took Matthew and me camping. My mother loathes being outside. She adores her comforts, but my father was content anywhere."

"We must all be able to take care of ourselves," Lady M said. "You never know what situations life will toss you into to see if you sink or swim. Whatever happens, you make the best of it."

Lady M had been widowed some time ago, and although she put on a brave face, I wondered if she missed her late husband.

"Well, I must retire. I have a busy day tomorrow, and unlike you young things, I can't function without an adequate amount of sleep." Lady M gave me a pointed look. "I'm sure you have much to discuss."

"I want to hear all about your suspects," Ruby said, once we'd bid Lady M goodnight.

"The list gets trickier by the day," I admitted. "What began as a possible natural death has turned into a definite murder by poison. And now, Iris's stabbing! It's so inconvenient. She was my prime suspect!"

"You're lucky your injuries weren't more serious," Ruby said, glancing at my midsection.

"Whoever it was didn't intend to kill me, but they wanted me out of the way long enough to escape. A slash of a blade certainly distracted me. As did Benji's injury."

"You should get weapons training," Ruby said. "Carry a concealed weapon, so you're ready the next time you're attacked."

"I'd rather not carry a gun in my handbag. Even the lightest would be tiresome." I shook my head. "I can deal with any troublemaker with my fists and fleet of foot."

"Not tonight, you didn't!" Ruby sighed. "You find yourself in increasingly perilous situations because I'm not there to support you."

"I have Benji. And when Jacob's in town, he's always willing to lend a hand. Besides, you're not in any condition to assist."

"I must be able to do something," Ruby insisted.

"I believe some men find a woman with child attractive," I said. "You could flirt with Detective Chief Inspector Taylor to distract him from having me arrested again."

She huffed. "That man is a fool."

"At least we agree on something."

"We agree on many things," Ruby said after a second of silence. "Although only when you're around, which is barely ever. I understand your situation tonight, but you can't keep making excuses not to see me. If you no longer wish our friendship to continue, then you must say so."

"It's not that." I took a steadying sip of tea, giving myself a few seconds to cut through the stiff awkwardness that had settled over us.

"Then what is it?" Ruby asked. "You only came back to London because Lady M sought you out and told you I was at death's door."

"Which was something of an exaggeration," I said.

"She didn't think you'd come otherwise."

"I was working my way towards it," I said. "I'll admit, it was a shock to learn of your condition. But the bigger shock was that you hid so much from me. You vanished! I was terribly concerned."

"You must understand I needed time to think, to figure things out for myself. I'm sorry for lying to you about where I was and what I was doing. But you know what you can be like."

"Practical and efficient?" I suggested.

"Bossy and controlling!"

I sniffed. "Oh, so that's how you see me?"

"That attitude is exactly why I needed time to myself. I had to figure things out without anyone's influence. Not from you, my family, or any of our friends."

"What about the chap who got you in the family way?" I asked. "Does he not have a say in any of this?"

"He's not important. He never was. And he won't be in the future."

"Was it that Italian fellow you nearly married?" I asked. "Did you reconnect with him?"

"Absolutely not. I'd never go near him again, even if he were the last man on Earth," Ruby said. "Fool me once, and all that. If you must know, it was an old rogue from the past. He's producing a play in London, and he invited me for a drink. We reminisced for hours, and after a few too many glasses of champagne, well, I rather got carried away."

I arched an eyebrow. "Did you get carried away only once?"

Ruby slapped a hand on her thigh. "More than once. He was charming! And devilishly handsome. I visited him several times."

"And each time there was reminiscing and plenty of champagne?"

"No judgy tones. I'm a single lady, and these are modern times."

"Indeed, they are. And I'm not judging, merely securing the facts."

Ruby's bottom lip jutted out. "By the time I realised I was with child, his play had moved to another city, and he'd left without saying a word."

"Do you not think he'd be interested in the child?"

"Not for a second. He's unreliable. Handsome, charming, good with words but with not a sensible thought in his head," Ruby said with a reassuring air of finality. "He's not in the picture, and I don't want him to be. That's not the sort of influence I want for my child."

I kept my tone neutral to avoid being called bossy. "I understand. So... what happens next?"

"Lady M has said I can live here for as long as I like," Ruby said. "Not in the main house, of course, but a workers' cottage has become free, so I'm to have that."

"That's splendid news. I'm glad you gave up your flat," I said. "It was no place to raise an infant. I always thought it smelled damp."

"It was damp. Some of my clothes were ruined," Ruby said. "Lady M has also offered me part-time work. It's not much, but it's something, so I'll have an income."

"I'm happy things are working out so well for you," I said sincerely.

The colour drained from Ruby's face. She placed a hand on her stomach and moaned softly.

I shot up and moved to sit beside her on the chaise longue. "You're running a fever. How long has this been going on?"

"It comes and goes," she whispered. "No one ever told me carrying a child would be so taxing on the body. I don't feel like myself. One minute I'm full of energy, and the next, it feels as though every ounce of strength has drained from me, and I can barely lift a finger."

I clasped her clammy hand and gave it a reassuring squeeze. "Is there anything I can do?"

"You can accept my apology and start being my friend again." Ruby closed her eyes just as a tear trickled from the corner of one eye. "I'm terrified of what the future holds. I don't know the first thing about raising a child. My parents were laissez faire and let us run wild. You can see how well that turned out. I'm unmarried and pregnant. Most of my siblings have scattered across the globe, and one brother was accused of murder not so long ago. We're dreadful role models."

"Nonsense. You have a free spirit, a generous heart, and you're clever." I brushed the tear away with a finger. "You're also clever enough to exploit your physical gifts to get your own way."

"I don't have the faintest idea what you're talking about." A small smile crept across Ruby's face as she reached up to adjust her hair. "But we work with what we're given. Although I sometimes wish I had your brain."

"It is not without its trials." I firmly clasped Ruby's hand, wanting her to know I was there for her and always would be. "You've been a nincompoop over this whole situation, but I understand why. And people have made me aware more than once that I can be a bit bossy, and I take control of situations. Perhaps I would have reacted out of shock when you told me the news and tried to control every detail of your impending motherhood, rather than giving you space."

Ruby opened her eyes and stared at me levelly. "We know each other so well."

"We do. And I'm glad of it. You had every right to hide. I can be a horror."

"A horror you may be, but you're my horrific best friend, and I've missed you dreadfully."

I blinked away my own tears. "We can't have that. I hope you accept my apology. I shouldn't have stayed away so long. Not when you're so unwell."

"I always feel better when you and Benji are here," Ruby said. "I should ask Lady M to make you up a guest room, and then you never have to leave."

"As much fun as that would be, my mother would faint at the very thought of me abandoning her. But I shall visit daily," I replied. "Unless of course I'm locked up and charged with another crime."

"The next time that happens, I'll be there, babe in arms, fighting beside you every step of the way."

I chuckled. "Detective Chief Inspector Taylor won't know what's hit him."

"It'll be a dirty nappy if he isn't on his best behaviour from now on."

Benji lifted his head and rested it gently on Ruby's thigh, wagging his tail at the sight of two friends reunited.

I inspected Ruby's expanding waistline. "So, how will we go about raising this infant?"

"Don't bother yourself with that," Ruby said. "More importantly, how will we go about solving this double murder?"

"It was wonderful. Just like old times." I smiled into the telephone the next morning as I recounted my reconciliation with Ruby to Jacob.

"I'm glad you're friendly again," he said. "I hated seeing you so down."

"Everything's working out," I replied. "Ruby's health is stable, and I've not been charged with any further crimes. Although I'm quite certain Detective Chief Inspector Taylor is desperate to find something he can pin on me."

For the past fifteen minutes, I'd updated Jacob on the case and my situation with Ruby while we ate breakfast. Even though we were in different counties, we always had a breakfast call when we could. It ensured we stayed involved in each other's lives and kept our business affairs running smoothly. It was a perfectly practical arrangement.

"Detective Chief Inspector Taylor needs a good thrashing," Jacob grumbled.

"I'd rather enjoy seeing you do that to him," I said. "Although Lady M did a good enough job of humiliating him when she had me released. You should have seen her. She was magnificent."

"She's not a lady to be trifled with," Jacob said. "Neither are you, as Detective Chief Inspector Taylor must have come to realise."

"Before I forget," I said, "I wanted to ask you about Gilbert Renwick. You must have encountered him when you worked locally."

Jacob drew in a sharp breath. "Unfortunately, many times. What do you want with him?"

"He was bothering Maudie about Cora. I asked Uncle Harry about him, and he immediately warned me off."

"Gil Renwick is the worst type of person," Jacob said.

"What can you tell me about him?"

"Although we could never gather enough evidence to prove it, he's killed at least twice. We never had sufficient evidence to convict, but Gil loves to brag. Someone overheard him boasting about his achievements. When we questioned him, he laughed and told us good luck finding the evidence."

"Why did he kill?"

"He thinks he owns certain parts of London. Anyone who steps on his toes, he removes. He was also involved in prostitution. Last I heard, he was stepping back from that game."

"That's where Cora started her career. Iris too. Though both claimed to have left that life behind, they were still entertaining men for money."

"Your uncle is right. Stay as far away from Gil as you can," Jacob warned.

"But what if he's behind this? I can't believe Maudie's involved. She's made poor choices, but she's no killer. And Iris, well, she's dead now. Who's next?"

"Maybe you, if you're not careful. I should leave Kent and assist you with this investigation."

"As much as I'd adore having you here, you can't abandon the fraud case. People are depending on you. And think of our business's reputation. We can't afford to let it slide."

"I'm thinking about the safety of someone I'm very fond of," Jacob said softly.

I smiled to myself. "Who might that be? Have you got a new fancy woman?"

"I know what you're like. You'll waltz into this situation and demand answers from Gil, but that's not how you handle a man like him. He's sly and quick with a blade."

"If his weapon of choice is a knife," I said thoughtfully, "then it's even more likely he was involved in Iris's murder."

"Veronica, you must be careful. Work closely with the police on this. Don't go it alone."

"I would if I could. But the only thing Detective Chief Inspector Taylor is interested in is locking me up. He's certainly not interested in solving the case. The police are of no use. Well, Sergeant Matthers is. I'll speak to him and see if he can assist."

"Don't put him in a difficult position, or he'll lose his job."

"I'll be discreet. I always am," I said. "But I need to learn more about Iris and Cora's backgrounds."

"How do you plan on doing that?" Jacob asked.

"I'm taking a trip to Belgravia. Although I need a little help to do so."

Chapter 15

"After the way you treated me, you're fortunate I even took your telephone call." Camille Hartley stepped out of the shadows, making me jump.

"I did apologise for thinking you were a killer," I said.

"It didn't feel particularly heartfelt," Camille replied coolly. Her gaze flicked over my plain dark coat. "Didn't I tell you to dress up? Belgravia isn't a place one wears working women's clothing."

"This is my finest wool coat," I retorted.

"The hem around one cuff is frayed," Camille pointed out. "At least you didn't bring your dog with you."

"Benji fits in anywhere, but I felt he'd draw too much attention, and he's recovering from an injury, so is staying with a friend."

"As adorable as your dog is, he'd have blown our cover. This brothel is upper class. It only accepts a certain type of clientele, and they're used to seeing their women refined, well-dressed, and not dragging a creature around on a lead."

"I never drag Benji anywhere." I glowered at her. "I thought the men expected to see the women mainly undressed."

"Some of that goes on, too," Camille said. "But the gentlemen who frequent the Belgravia Club want more than exposed flesh. They like intelligent conversation, good-quality alcohol, and stimulation of varying sorts."

"I can certainly offer them intelligent conversation, but they'll get nothing else from me," I said. "I've got a nice dress on underneath this coat."

Camille pursed her lips. "You'll have to do. And we need to hurry. My inside connection has left us a back entrance open, but she's not sure how long it'll remain unnoticed. We'll slip inside, head along the corridor, and watch the goings-on. That'll give you the insight you're after about Cora and Iris."

I'd been in two minds when I'd reached out to Camille about arranging a visit to the Belgravia brothel, but I needed to know more about the victims. I was certain their murders were connected. I just didn't yet know what that connection was.

"As you can see, the club is popular." Camille paused beside me as a private car pulled up outside an ornate front door. Four men in tuxedos tumbled out, laughing and back-slapping one another. A well-dressed butler in a traditional suit and white gloves opened the door, spilling light out into the evening.

"Everything inside is first class," Camille said. "That was how Cora designed it. She didn't want the rough clientele. They ruined the business, the girls, and barely paid a penny for the services offered. She targeted men in business, industry, theatre, and even royalty."

"That makes sound business sense." I followed Camille along a tidy back passage towards a crack of light beneath a door.

"Imagine the scoop if we discover a member of the royal family inside," Camille whispered. "I could write for any newspaper in the country and name my price."

"That is, if the royal family ever allowed the story to come to light," I said. "They're known for squashing scandals when they threaten their image."

Camille wrinkled her nose. "True enough. Some of the things alleged about royalty turn even the most hardened stomach. Still, maybe we'll get lucky tonight. What do you say?"

"I say we go in, remain discreet, and speak to your contact."

"She'll be busy since she's working, but I'll see if we can steal five minutes."

We slipped inside. Crates and bottles of alcohol lined the corridor, all neatly arranged. The faint scent of smoke and expensive perfume hung in the air.

"Be on your guard once we step into the open," Camille warned. "It's not uncommon for some men to bring their wives, but two ladies alone will draw attention. Blend in as much as you can." Her gaze flicked over my coat again.

"Why would a wife wish to visit such an establishment with her husband?" I asked.

"To give herself a break from wifely bedroom duties. Or perhaps they get a peculiar thrill from it. Some have tastes they wish to indulge. That's not for us to judge."

"Fair point," I murmured. "I'll do my best to blend in."

Camille smirked and stopped beside a closed door. "It's time to enter the zoo." She pulled it open.

A waft of music, sweet-scented air, and laughter flooded over me as I stared into a large open space.

There was a stage at the front, several smaller raised platforms where women danced, and many doors leading off the main area. The décor was sparkle, shimmer, and shine, with a hefty chandelier dominating the ceiling. Red velvet cloth covered the tables, and crystal vases held lilies and roses. Everything gleamed with wealth and indulgence.

"Why is there so much security?" I whispered as we edged closer to the main floor. I counted a dozen well-dressed, broad-shouldered chaps stationed discreetly around the perimeter, watching everything.

"The madam keeps things respectable. If anyone causes trouble, they're out on their ear."

"Who is the new madam?"

"Genevieve Granger. She's been in charge since Cora left. She trained under Cora, so she knows all the tricks."

"Perhaps Cora never really gave up the business," I murmured. "She simply expanded her reach."

"There's my contact." Camille discreetly raised a hand.

A scantily dressed woman with a full face of makeup approached in a bustier and silk stockings, covered by a sheer wrap. It wasn't until she drew closer that I recognised her.

My mouth fell open. "Isabella? You work here?"

She frowned and looked about quickly. "Hush! In here, I'm known as Octavia Demure. Don't laugh. The madam picked the name for me. We all have exotic names. It's what the gentlemen like."

"Have things got so tough for you that you need a job here?" I asked.

"Don't be so naïve, Veronica," she hissed. "I'm undercover. And I'm just serving drinks. Although the madam is becoming insistent I get more involved. I may have to escape before things become difficult."

"You're undercover to break a story?" I asked.

"Why else would I be here? You seem to think you're the only one who can make a name for yourself in the newspaper business. Camille and I do just fine, as you can see."

I glanced at Camille, who gave a small shrug. Isabella had struggled to gain respect in the field of journalism. Instead of being given a chance to develop as a serious journalist, she was sent on demeaning errands such as fetching birthday gifts for her editor's wife.

"Thanks for getting us in," Camille said.

"When you told me Iris had been murdered, I was stunned. When she got out of the game, she was a useful source of information," Isabella said.

"You're writing an exposé about this place?" I asked.

"We formed an alliance to expose this industry's tawdriness." Isabella nodded at Camille.

"Initially, I was interested in Cora's fashion knowledge, but I soon realised I had a much bigger story. That was where Isabella came in," Camilla said. "I'm still in two minds if we should carry on. Especially now that girls are being murdered."

"That's all the more reason to do it." Isabella adjusted her bustier. "I've been working on this piece for ages, but didn't have enough clout to get things moving. Then Camille told me about her work with Cora, and it fit together."

I wasn't jealous. If they pulled this off, it would be the making of them.

"I can't talk for long. There are always eyes on you," Isabella said. "Order drinks. If you don't, there'll be questions. And don't be cheap about it."

"We'll have champagne," I said. "Whatever's the most expensive, so you give us extra special attention."

Isabella nodded her approval and disappeared into the crowd.

"We've got an interesting mix in tonight," Camille murmured, tugging me towards a shadowy corner where a small table waited. "Over there, that's a Swedish duke, and possibly his brother, judging by how alike they are. To their right is the chief executive of one of the country's largest banking firms. And see him in the white tuxedo? That's a steel magnate. He must be down from the North for a little London entertainment."

I studied the men. Each had at least one woman in attendance, often more. The Swedish duke had a striking redhead seated on his lap, wearing little more than a slip and a string of pearls. Her arms were draped around his neck as she whispered into his ear. Whatever she said made him grin broadly before he gave her a playful pat on the behind.

"Oh, my! There's Lady Fairfax's son," Camille added. "I thought she'd banned him from this sort of nonsense."

"Lady Fairfax... I've heard that name before," I said. "She sent her chauffeur into the Rusty Nail. He was looking for her son."

Camille nodded. "Tarquin Fairfax. He built quite a nasty reputation before he'd even turned twenty. He inherited a substantial sum far too young and was abysmally educated in how to manage it. Blew through vast amounts before his mother stepped in."

"And spent a fair portion of it in brothels?" I guessed.

"Some of it, most certainly, in here. He's riddled with addiction. Drinks like a fish, never wears the same outfit twice, and travels constantly. He's purchased houses for several of his close female friends, furnishing them extravagantly and hosting lavish parties."

"I vaguely remember an article we published about the Fairfax family," I said. "Something about Tarquin retreating to a private institution for a health condition."

"He experienced nervous exhaustion," Camille said, lowering her voice, "after some secret scandal in his early twenties."

"A scandal involving this place?" I asked.

"It's possible," Camille replied. "The fearsome Lady Eugenia Fairfax was appalled and humiliated when she learned of her son's disgraceful behaviour. She wasn't about to let the family name be dragged through the mud. I'd wager she had him institutionalised while she decided what to do next."

"Gosh. You hear of that happening to women who don't toe the line, but it's not so common for a man."

"The Fairfax family owns half of Cornwall and Devon. They have ties to royalty. If she wanted her son put away to tame his wildness, she'd have done it without a moment's hesitation to protect the family reputation." Camille glanced over as a bray of laughter drifted towards us from Tarquin Fairfax's table. "It seems she hasn't quite tamed him yet."

"She'll be livid if she learns he's here," I said. "When her chauffeur came to the Rusty Nail, it sounded as though Tarquin had been missing for some time."

"Perhaps he escaped the shackles or bribed his way free," Camille said. "He's not entirely out of funds."

Isabella returned with our champagne and two flutes. She poured with grace, though she paused mid-pour as a sudden shout rang out across the room, followed by the shatter of glass.

Two suited men sprang into action, dashing across the floor to attend to the disturbance. They gathered up the drunkard who'd made a spectacle of himself and dragged him swiftly through a side door.

"They're efficient at dealing with trouble here," I remarked as Isabella finished pouring.

"The madam looks after everyone," Isabella said. "She's strict, but she watches out for her girls. She won't stand for anybody being harmed. If there's any nonsense, the men are out the door and banned for life. People who come here know the rules, and those who don't, learn them quickly, or they don't come back."

"And here is the lady in question." Camille nodded towards a door that had just swung open.

A tall, willowy brunette emerged, gliding across the floor in a red silk dress that plunged daringly at the neckline and shimmered with every step. Jewels sparkled at her throat and ears, and a plume of feathers crowned her hair. She moved with a languid grace, stopping to speak with each gentleman, accepting kisses to her hand, sips of their drinks, and offering measured laughter in return.

It was difficult to determine her exact age in the dim lighting, but I'd have placed her in her late twenties. She exuded the calm confidence of a woman who understood precisely how the world worked and how to bend it to her will. She paused by one of her security men, murmured something to him, and he hastened away through the door she'd emerged from.

"Genevieve is something else," Camille whispered. "She came from nothing. Raised by a family of travelling gypsies, if the stories are to be believed."

"And rumour has it," Isabella lowered her voice as she hovered beside us, "that her Wiccan grandmother gifted her eternal beauty and long life. Everyone who meets Genevieve falls under her spell and gives her whatever she desires."

"Wouldn't that be nice?" I murmured. "She has a beguiling way about her."

"She even charms the girls," Isabella said. "Although if she catches me shirking my duties, I'll be in trouble. I'd better go." And with that, she darted away.

"Let's stay in the shadows for now," Camille advised. "Watch how things operate. Isabella said she'd speak to some of the girls, see if any will talk about Iris and Cora."

"I'm already learning a great deal just by being here," I said. "If Cora established a place like this, she clearly had intelligence and charm on par with Genevieve."

"Not quite enough to prevent herself from being poisoned," Camille replied.

A shout caught my attention. I turned to see the security man who'd gone into Genevieve's room return, his shoulders hunched and hands fisted. He gestured to his similarly suited colleagues to join him. Why did he need backup?

A moment later, Gilbert Renwick marched out of the room and over to Genevieve, shouted something in her face, then stormed away.

"Oh dear." Camille's eyes narrowed. "If Genevieve is associating with the likes of Gil Renwick, she doesn't have things as organised as she'd like everyone to believe."

"You're familiar with Gil's activities?"

"Who isn't?"

"I wasn't until recently. But this is a stroke of luck. That's just the fellow I need to speak to." I stood. "Let's go. It's time I had a word with Mr Renwick."

Chapter 16

"I'm always one for an adventure," Camille said as she hurried along with me to the exit, "but perhaps we should get the authorities involved. Gil Renwick isn't someone I want paying me any attention."

I kept focussed on Gil as we emerged from the warm, smoky brothel. "We'll keep our distance."

"You said you wanted to speak with him," Camille said. "How do you plan to do that? Telepathically?"

"Even I know not to tackle a man whose anger is so easily roused." I winced as Gil punched a billboard. He followed that act of senseless violence by kicking a bin and scattering the contents across the street before stomping through it. "It's no wonder he's so well known to the police. His temper is out of control."

"He's rumoured to have killed." Camille gripped my elbow. "We should go back to the club. Perhaps we can get some answers from Genevieve about why he was so angry."

"I doubt she'll talk to two journalists. Let's keep on his tail for a few minutes and see where he goes."

"You'll get me in trouble." Camille still followed me, but we maintained our distance as Gil terrified some innocent passers-by with a roaring howl as they hurried by.

"Gil was looking for Cora at the Rusty Nail," I said. "Now he's at the brothel confronting Genevieve. His concerns must relate to the club."

"Was that concern worth killing for?" Camille grimaced. "I'm too afraid to ask him that question."

"I'm not afraid of a bully," I said.

"Be afraid of this one. He has no conscience or soul," Camille said.

Gil stopped at the corner, seeming to deliberate which way to go.

I gently tugged Camille into a nearby alley so we wouldn't be spotted. A moment later, a car pulled to a stop beside him. The driver climbed out just as the back window slid down.

"I recognise that chauffeur!" I said. "That's Lady Fairfax's driver. Is Gil working for the Fairfax family?"

There was a terse conversation then Gil drew back from the car and kicked it. A second later, the chauffeur zoomed off, leaving Gil yelling after them.

"My word!" Camille said. "I wasn't expecting that."

I nodded, my eyebrows raised. "We've certainly got more questions than answers, but what a night!"

The next morning, I was up bright and early, making a most important telephone call.

"Of course I know Lady Fairfax! I know all the notable women in this area. What do you want with her?" Lady M asked.

"I need to ask you a favour," I said. "Lady Fairfax's son could be connected to what happened in the case I'm investigating."

"Tell me everything."

I didn't hide my smile. Sometimes, Lady M reminded me of my dear, frustrating, eternally nosy mother.

I filled in the gaps, ending with, "Last night, I saw Lady Fairfax speaking to a man of ill repute."

"How exciting! Do tell more."

"I can do more than that," I said. "If you would be so good as to arrange an afternoon tea, I'll conduct some discreet questioning."

"You want to conduct an undercover operation in my home?" Lady M sounded thrilled.

"Your influence and exclusive invitation will guarantee Lady Fairfax visits at short notice."

"My word! You want to do it today?"

"If you can fit in a touch of sleuthing before teatime, I'd appreciate it."

"Say no more. This is exhilarating!" Lady M said. "And Ruby will be so thrilled."

"She's welcome to be there, but how will you explain her condition to Lady Fairfax?"

"Don't concern yourself with that. We've been making plans. I'll contact Lady Fairfax immediately and demand her company," Lady M said. "She's a lady of leisure and always complains of being bored, so I'm sure a last-minute event will excite her just as much as it will me. I'll see you here at three o'clock."

Delighted my plan was coming together so neatly, I dashed to work and whizzed through an enormous pile of obituaries in record time. And I was glad I did, because not only would I need to leave work early for our tea and questions, but I also planned to take an extended lunch break to visit Maudie.

Ignoring Bob's grumbles, I shot off on the dot of noon, heading directly for the police station. I was in such a hurry as I raced through the main doors that I collided with Father Kersey. I bounced off his chest with an audible gasp, making my recently dislocated shoulder twinge in protest.

"Oh, my dear lady, I must apologise." He reached out to steady me.

"That was entirely my fault. I wasn't looking where I was going," I said. "I'm eager to see Maudie. Have you been to visit her?"

"Indeed, I have." He let out a sigh and shook his head. "I fear there's little I can do to ease her suffering."

"I'm doing plenty. She won't suffer for long. Maudie is innocent."

"I admire your naïve innocence. But Maudie has a troubled past."

"Whatever that trouble was, she's left it behind," I said. "She's a reformed character."

"There are so many of you out there who need my services," Father Kersey continued, as if I hadn't spoken. "I look after a shelter for fallen women, and we're always looking for able-bodied volunteers. If ever you have spare time, you could share your own story." His gaze flicked to my bare ring finger.

"I shall consult my calendar," I retorted. "But independence and a free spirit aren't marks of a fallen woman."

He gently patted my arm. "Good day to you."

I glanced over my shoulder at Father Kersey. I admired him for assisting the fallen women, as he called them, but we shouldn't live in a society where anyone fell, or was poor, or needed help. After the Great War, this country had boomed, so why hadn't it picked everybody up and carried them along to prosperity?

After checking at the desk and ensuring I had a visitor's pass, I was escorted to see Maudie in her cell. Unfortunately, there were no available interview rooms, so I had to speak to her through the closed door.

We exchanged a few pleasantries, and I checked to ensure she had everything she needed, but Maudie was of little help and had no knowledge of Tarquin visiting the Rusty Nail when Cora had been staying there.

After promising her I'd have new information soon, I left with an air of determination. This connection to the Fairfax family looked promising, and I'd soon be bringing Maudie home.

After putting in another hour of work at the London Times, I dashed to Lady M's estate. I'd even taken a few moments to tidy my appearance, given I was indulging in finger sandwiches and delicious cake with such esteemed company.

I was ten minutes early, which gave me ample opportunity to find the best position to seat myself and learn exactly how Lady M planned to introduce Ruby.

"I'm a distant relative, although we won't say what kind." Ruby was already polishing off a piece of iced lemon cake. "Lady M will say she took me in when she felt sorry for me after my husband died in the war."

"It's a plausible story," I said.

"I feel a touch guilty, though, since that happened to so many women, and they're less fortunate than I am. But I don't want to be shut away like some dirty little secret. And I'm so excited to be involved in the investigation," Ruby said.

There was a knock at the front door.

"We won't have to wait long to get answers. That must be Lady Fairfax," I said. I patted Benji's head, happy to see him so content after I'd left him with Ruby to rest and recover. No doubt, the copious amount of treats Ruby fed him led to such a cheerful disposition.

Lady M joined us a few seconds later, wearing a tailored green dress made of a silk blend crepe, with diamonds in her earlobes. "Is everything in order?" She settled herself with precision on the velvet sofa.

"Yes. I'll say I'm writing a piece about up-and-coming young bachelors," I said. "I'm hoping Lady Fairfax will see this as positive publicity for her wayward son and open up. I'll mention the no-doubt unfounded rumours of his bad behaviour and work hard to convince her I don't believe a word of it."

Lady M smirked. "Lady Fairfax is no fool. She appreciates plain talk. Less flattery and more fact is the ideal way to address her."

Before we could further discuss the best approach, there was a knock at the door, and the butler escorted Lady Fairfax in. Introductions were made, and Lady Fairfax settled into a seat, sweeping her wide skirt expertly around her ankles. In a similar style to Lady M, she wore a buttoned-up silk dress and pearls rather than diamonds.

"I was most surprised and delighted to receive such a last-minute invitation," she said. "You're usually far too busy for casual company."

Lady M smiled sweetly. "It's a flaw in my character I am rectifying. And of course, I wished to assist my young friend. Veronica was eager to meet you."

As tea was poured and cakes and sandwiches distributed by the efficient serving staff, Lady Fairfax continued. "I would have appreciated notice as to the questions you wish to ask about my family. But Marie Antoinette assured me you are of reputable standing."

"The London Times only prints the truth," I said.

Lady Fairfax hesitated before sipping from a delicate teacup. "So few do."

"I heard some rumours about your son," I added. "This article will help to redress them."

"Rumours must always be ignored." Lady Fairfax inspected a delicate macaroon and wrinkled her nose as though it offended her. "My son had a comprehensive education. He was schooled at Oxford, which is a fine college."

"It is the making of most young men and women, too," I said. "They've recently opened the doors to female scholars."

"I'm not sure what I think about that," Lady Fairfax replied. "We have a duty as wives and mothers."

"Not all of us can be so fortunate as to fulfil that duty," Lady M said. "Veronica, ask your questions about Tarquin. We're both busy. Then perhaps I can show you the new portraits in the gallery, Eugenia?"

"How delightful. Go ahead," Lady Fairfax said.

"Let's begin with the rumours and get that nasty business out of the way, so I ensure I have everything correct," I said.

"If we must," Lady Fairfax replied. "But why waste our time by beginning with falsehoods?"

"It's just for my records. One of my connections mentioned Tarquin frequents gentlemen's clubs. Is there any truth in that?"

Lady Fairfax tensed in her chair. "None whatsoever. Ask another question. A smarter one."

"What about visiting a certain well-known brothel in Belgravia?"

"I didn't know there was such a thing, and if there is, there shouldn't be." Lady Fairfax set down her plate. "I'd rather not continue with this manner of questioning. It's inappropriate."

"Veronica knows what she's doing," Lady M said. "I'd be thrilled if she were interviewing me, but my life has become terribly dull, so I have nothing of interest to share."

Lady Fairfax sighed, her gaze shifting to Ruby, whose appetite had returned with full force, and she was on her third plate of sandwiches. "Continue."

It was time to get to the point. "Did you enjoy your late-night drive yesterday?"

"I don't drive," Lady Fairfax said, frowning.

"My apologies. Let me be more specific. Did you enjoy the late-night drive your chauffeur conducted? It was around Belgravia, I believe."

"Is this woman of sound mind?" Lady Fairfax turned to Lady M. "What do my travel plans have to do with

Tarquin's eligibility as an up-and-coming bachelor of note?"

"Perhaps it would be wise to answer the question, and then you'll find out," Lady M said.

"I wasn't in Belgravia last night. I've no reason to be there. I prefer a more established part of London." Lady Fairfax regarded me with suspicion. "Actually, I'm not fond of London at all. It's too easy for our children to get led astray with all the available social activities."

"Is that what happened with Tarquin?" I asked. "He discovered the brothel in Belgravia and was entranced?"

Lady Fairfax stood abruptly and flung down her napkin. "This is an outrage! You want to know nothing of Tarquin's true nature and wish only to dig into the rumours. None of it is true! And if I see a word about him printed in that rag of a newspaper of yours, I shall sue."

"Calm yourself," Lady M said. "And sit down. Try the lemon slice. It's delicious."

"I have no appetite," Lady Fairfax replied.

"It really is delightful," Ruby said, her mouth full of cake.

Lady Fairfax's lips curled. "Despite you being in the family way, you still must watch your figure."

Ruby swallowed her large mouthful of cake, a faint blush rising to her cheeks.

"Veronica is a sensible sort and helpful," Lady M said. "We both know Tarquin has got himself into a pickle. Veronica wants to fix that."

Lady Fairfax glared at me. "How can she fix Tarquin? No one can."

Lady M sipped from a fine china teacup. She nodded to me. "Sharing the situation may result in a successful outcome."

After a period of tense silence, Lady Fairfax fiddling with her cup, her pearls, and finally her sleeves, she sighed. "Tarquin is missing."

"And you're searching for him in his favourite haunts?" I asked. "One of them being the gentlemen's club in Belgravia."

"How do you know that?" Lady Fairfax asked.

"Your chauffeur was seen in Belgravia and at a pub where the late Cora Bellamy set up a temporary... shop."

"My chauffeur may go where he pleases when he's off duty," Lady Fairfax retorted.

"Why was he asking about Tarquin if he was off duty?" I asked. "You do know Cora Bellamy was murdered, don't you?"

"I heard something of the sort," Lady Fairfax said coldly.

"And another of her girls was stabbed to death recently. I fear there is a connection."

Lady Fairfax paled. She didn't speak for at least a minute. "You can't imagine it was Tarquin."

"As charming as your son is, he acts before he thinks," Lady M said. "Speaking plainly, that was how he frittered away so much of his fortune. He sees something, and he takes it or buys it without a second to consider the consequences."

"I overindulged him when he was young," Lady Fairfax said with some reluctance. "But that doesn't make him a bad person. Yes, Tarquin got into trouble now and again, but nothing of such a serious nature."

"Has he ever got girls in trouble?" I asked.

Lady Fairfax's hand trembled as she set down her teacup. "I have assisted some young ladies who found themselves with child. I find a payment enough to stop them gossiping that the child could be Tarquin's. And I give them enough to set up a home far from here. I always encourage the South coast, since the sea air is good for children."

"Sometimes one has to do such things," Lady M said. "We have reputations to maintain."

Ruby placed a hand protectively over her stomach and focussed on her plate of cake.

Lady Fairfax lowered her gaze. "I must stop Tarquin from being enticed back into that scene. Those girls are devious, and his will is weak."

"Tarquin is an adult," Lady M said. "He's responsible for his choices. If he spent his fortune on frippery and fancy women, no one forced him to do it."

Lady Fairfax frowned, but her ire faded as her shoulders sank. "I am at a loss for what to do. He isn't perfect, but he's still my son."

"I won't write anything bad about Tarquin," I said. "But I must ensure he hasn't got himself embroiled in this terrible business."

Lady M leant over and patted Lady Fairfax's arm. "Trust Veronica. You've been so worried about him. Let us assist you."

Lady Fairfax gathered herself, the blue-blood steely resolve straightening her spine as she met my gaze.

"Very well. I will tell you what I know. Tarquin has been missing for some time," Lady Fairfax said. "I've looked in the places he frequents, but he's disappeared.

I'm convinced he left London, which means he had nothing to do with what happened to those women."

"Perhaps he's not missing, but he's avoiding you because he's hiding a secret," I suggested.

"That secret won't be murder!" Lady Fairfax smoothed her skirt. "Of course, one wonders if those girls brought it upon themselves, given the work they did."

"Perhaps they had no choice but to do that work," I replied. "Many people aren't born into wealth and don't have unlimited funds to spend carelessly, unconcerned about the repercussions of their actions because they know money can fix their problems."

"There's no need for that!" Lady Fairfax stood abruptly. "It's time I left."

"What if I told you I saw Tarquin?" I asked. "He was at the Belgravia club last night."

Lady Fairfax speared me with a death glare. "Then I would say you're a liar. I do not require help. The situation is under control. Tarquin has left London, so stop meddling in his affairs. Good afternoon." She turned and left the room.

We waited in silence until the front door closed.

I let out a sigh, annoyed I'd allowed my dislike of Lady Fairfax's privileged tongue and easy dismissal of Cora and Iris to spill out.

"If it wasn't Tarquin, then Lady Fairfax has a motive to kill," Ruby said. "The look she gave you just before she left sent a chill down my spine."

"Lady Fairfax is no killer," Lady M said.

"Maybe not directly," I said. "But what if she paid Gil Renwick to commit the crimes?"

We considered the options while we devoured the remaining miniature sandwiches and cake. Lady Fairfax had no control over her son and no ability to tame his wild ways. He was a suspect. And now, so was she.

By the time I left, Ruby was yawning, ready for a pre-dinner nap, so I didn't linger, glad she could get some rest after a solid meal had gone down.

I spent the evening with my mother and Matthew before heading up to get some much-needed shut-eye of my own.

It took me a while to drift off, my head full of murder suspects. I'd left Benji with Ruby, since they were doing each other good, so I didn't have his comforting presence.

I was just dozing when a floorboard creaked. I flipped onto my back and opened my eyes.

There was another creak, this time closer.

My breath stuttered as a shadowy figure loomed over me, a knife glinting in one hand.

Chapter 17

Despite the threat of a blade so close to my throat, I refused to panic. That would only provoke the intruder to do the same, and a panicked individual wielding a weapon was the last thing I needed.

I had to remain as calm as possible. "There is money in my handbag, and a small amount of jewellery in the top drawer behind you. Take it and leave."

"I ain't here to thieve."

My heart jumped. I recognised that voice. "Is that you, Gil?" I kept my voice low, so as not to wake Matthew or my mother. I had no wish to involve them in this unpleasant business.

"Only my friends call me that, and we ain't friends." He grunted, and the blade inched closer to my throat.

"Did Lady Fairfax send you to warn me off?" I asked. "You're working for her, aren't you?"

"I only work for myself," he replied, his voice a low rumble. "You need to stop poking about in business that don't concern you."

"If you're referring to Cora Bellamy's murder, then it very much concerns me, considering her body was found in my pub," I said. "Murdering one of my guests is the height of bad manners, and it will do nothing for the pub's reputation."

"You think that was me?" Gil asked.

"I'm aware you had an association with Cora and her brothel."

"She don't own that place no more," Gil said.

"Yet you're still interested in it," I replied. "Did you enjoy your recent visit?"

His teeth glinted in the gloom. "How do you know so much about me?"

"I pay attention. And I intend to get to the bottom of this mystery. Well, there are now two mysteries to contend with, thanks to you."

"I don't know what you're talking about, missus. But this is your only warning," Gil said. "I could've stabbed you while you slept. I watched you for a while. Couldn't get comfortable. Got something on your mind, have you?"

"Two murders in such a short amount of time would trouble most people," I said. "Unless they're accustomed to that sort of thing. How many murders have you committed, Gil?"

"Mind your business. I'm not telling some nosey old shrew anything."

I glanced at the knife. It was long and thin, with a serrated edge meant to go in deep and maximise damage. I intended to avoid being struck by it at all costs.

"Got you scared, ain't I?" he said. "So you should be. Stay away from Belgravia. It's no place for you."

"It was a place for Cora and Iris for many years," I said. "There's history there. History that could help me solve these crimes."

"Iris? Do you mean Iris Dane?"

"She worked at the brothel too," I said. "Do you know Iris?"

"Of course I do," he replied.

"She's the other woman who was recently murdered," I said.

The sound that came out of Gil had me wondering if he'd been punched in the kidney. He lowered the blade and rocked back on his heels. "Iris is dead?"

I used his distraction to launch out of bed. The moment my feet hit the floor, I twisted to the side, catching the edge of the blanket and flinging it in his direction. It wasn't much, but it gave me the half-second I needed.

Gil swore as the fabric tangled around his arm, and I surged forward, aiming low. He wasn't expecting that.

I drove my shoulder into his midriff. He staggered backwards, but his grip on the knife held fast. I clawed at his wrist, fingers scrabbling for the weapon, but he was strong. Far stronger than I'd anticipated.

He yanked me sideways, trying to throw me off. I went with the motion, twisting, then brought my knee up sharply between us. It connected with a soft spot. He grunted and faltered.

With both hands, I seized Gil's arm, twisted it hard, and slammed my elbow into the joint. The knife dropped with a clatter. I kicked it under the bed.

Gil reached for me, but I ducked out of his grasp and planted a palm against his chest, pushing him back with all my strength.

"Have you lost your mind, taking a man's weapon?" he cried.

"I value my life," I said. "You needed to be disarmed."

"You could have got yourself killed." But Gil no longer seemed angry. In truth, he seemed upset.

"How well did you know Iris?" I remained standing, crouched and ready to bolt for the door at the first sign Gil's senses returned and he realised he didn't need a knife to kill me.

He rubbed a hand down his face and blew out a long breath. "I first met Iris in Belgravia. She was working the tables, but Cora soon got her involved in everything else. That's how those places work. They get the girls serving drinks and selling cigarettes then twist their arms and tell them how much more money they could make in the back rooms."

"You paid for Iris's services?" I asked.

"Not me," he growled, wiping the back of his hand across his eyes. "We were friendly. Like, we understood each other. We both came from rough backgrounds, and we... we got each other. I liked her."

"You really didn't know Iris was dead?" I asked.

"It's the first I've heard of it. I should know what's going on with my girl."

"Your girl? You were stepping out with Iris?" I asked.

"Stepping out," he said, shaking his head. "It's different for the likes of me and Iris. We grew up in the gutter, so we'll never be respectable. We do what we have to do to survive. There's no stepping out, or courtships, or meeting the parents. You get on with things. A lady like you wouldn't understand."

"I understand more than you know," I said. "Perhaps I had a more comfortable upbringing, but I've seen my fair share of hard times."

Gil grunted again, suggesting he didn't believe me.

"Perhaps you can help me figure out what happened to Iris," I said. "That's why I'm poking about, as you call it. And I must find out what happened to Cora, too. The police are mistaken in thinking my landlady had something to do with that death."

"I heard Cora was poisoned," Gil said. "Is that what happened to Iris?"

"She was stabbed. And since you broke into this house, wielding a knife and threatening me, you won't be surprised I thought you were involved."

"I'd never stab my girl," he said quietly. "We argued, but I always knew when to walk away. And I wouldn't stab a woman. Not really. It was just a threat to scare you enough to walk away."

"You've never stabbed a woman?" I asked. "Are you telling me the truth?"

He bared his teeth and smiled coldly. "Are you calling me a liar?"

I lifted my silken pyjama top a few inches to reveal the injury on my stomach. "You didn't do this when I visited Iris's salon? That was where I found her body."

He whistled low as he eyed the wound. "I always use serrated blades. And that cut wasn't meant to kill. When I stab, I aim for vital organs or a vein. That way, the bleeder's gone before anyone can help."

"How thoughtful of you," I said dryly.

Gil's faint smile faded. "Iris died in her salon? I still don't believe it. Are you sure it was her?"

"Quite sure," I said. "I was eager to speak to her because I thought she had murdered Cora."

"They had their problems. They were powerful women, both of them. That's why I liked Iris. She spoke her mind. Fearless. If she wanted something, she'd get it. When she left Belgravia, nothing Cora said could change her mind. Iris wanted a different life, so she went for it."

"It wasn't so different, though, was it?" I asked. "When I visited the salon, I noticed a gentleman being ushered down a side alley. I wonder why?"

Gil shrugged. "It's hard to break free when that's all you've known. And the money was good. Iris wanted to travel. We talked about seeing the world. I thought it was just talk at first, but the more she went on about it, the more I realised she was serious. She was saving hard." He sniffed. "And now she'll never go."

"I am sorry for your loss," I said gently.

"Few people understand me," he murmured. "But Iris was one of them."

"I'll speak plainly with you," I said. "I'm helping, not making trouble. I want to find out who killed Cora and Iris."

Gil narrowed his gaze. "How will you do that?"

"This isn't my first murder," I replied. "I believe they're connected. When I saw you at the Belgravia brothel and then speaking to Lady Fairfax, I put the pieces together and assumed you were dealing with her problems."

"Lady Fairfax hasn't ordered me to kill," Gil said. "She's paying me to find her idiot son. She heard I run a few gambling dens, and her snooty-nosed baby likes to lose all his money in them, so she paid me a few coins to let her know if he showed up."

"Did you tell her you saw him at the brothel?" I asked.

"I did. And she told me I was lying. I hate being called a liar. So, we had words. I told her where she could stick her deal, and she said she'd never been so insulted. I said I'd be happy to continue insulting her," he added with a dark grin, "and that's when the driver left."

"That was all she asked of you?" I said. "She didn't send you here to warn me off?"

"After we met at the Rusty Nail, I asked about you. I figured the fewer people with eyes on me, the better, and you'd be easy to scare off."

"I'm sorry you were so effortlessly fooled," I replied. "I'm not for scaring."

"I see that. I'll destroy whoever did this to Iris," Gil said, low and fierce. "She thought she'd landed on her feet, getting away from Cora. And yes, perhaps she took on a few extra clients, but it wasn't forever. She had a plan. We were going to be together, and now someone's taken that away." He huffed, grumbled to himself, and sniffed back more tears.

"What about Cora?" I asked. "Was she pressuring Iris to return to her Belgravia lifestyle? Both ladies had tempers."

"Cora let Iris go without much fuss, but she wasn't happy about it. Iris was one of her best girls."

"If Cora had kept the pressure up, Iris might have snapped," I said. "Iris killed Cora, and then someone killed Iris. That's the theory I'm working on."

"Iris would never do that. We needed Cora alive," Gil said.

"Why would that be?" I asked.

"You don't need all the details," he said, eyes narrowing. "Let's just say we had plans to make money off that twisted old crone."

"You had something on Cora?"

"She was a smart one. She taught Iris everything. Cora left no trail or evidence that she had done wrong. That's how she carried on in Belgravia for so long."

"She also carried on when she retired to my pub," I said. "That's how I knew there was a problem. My landlady contacted me and said Cora had been conducting business as usual."

He huffed a breath. "She was too long in the tooth to be lying on her back. Still, there's something to be said for a mature woman."

I pushed my luck. "How were you planning to make money off Cora?"

"You're getting nothing more out of me," Gil said. "But I want something from you. Or you'll find yourself in trouble."

"I believe I'm already in the middle of a troubling situation," I said. "Had I not disarmed you, I'd be bleeding out in my bed."

"No doubt you would. You've got a smart tongue. Not everyone likes that."

"My smart tongue has helped to solve crimes," I said evenly. "I make no apologies for it."

"You will help me," Gil demanded, "or else."

"Or else what?" I asked. "Do you plan on shooting me instead?"

Gil leant away and stared at me then barked out a short laugh. "You remind me of Iris. She was just as fearless."

"I'm not fearless," I said. "I take great care when a man is brandishing a weapon at me, but I am determined to get to the truth. What happened to Cora and Iris was wrong. The police aren't serving justice."

"I want nothing to do with the plod."

"I can be the go-between."

"You'll help?"

"I suggested the possibility first, so keep up, good fellow."

Gil's eyebrows shot up in surprise.

Now I had his attention and, seemingly, his cooperation, I shared more. "There's one thing I forgot to mention about Iris."

"What would that be?" Gil asked.

"I disturbed Iris's attacker, which is how I came by my injury. I contacted the police, but by the time they arrived, Iris's body was gone."

Gil's mouth dropped open in disbelief. "Those rotten toerags! Why take her body?"

"I can only assume to conceal evidence." I gave Gil a moment to collect himself. "Her body being taken is useful, though."

"How do you figure that?" Gil sniffed and wiped the back of his hand across his nose.

I reached into a drawer and extracted a cotton handkerchief for him. "There must be more than one killer, or our killer has an accomplice. They couldn't have rolled Iris's body in the rug she lay on and moved her alone. Not in the short time it took for the police to reach the scene. It would have taken two able-bodied, strong individuals."

"Those devils," Gil said darkly. "I'll skin them alive. They won't get away with this."

"We'll make sure they don't," I said.

"Then we're partners."

"If you answer me one thing honestly."

He glowered at me. "Don't you know who you're dealing with?"

"Very much so. You're a man of influence. But I'm not forgetting you're also a murder suspect. You threatened Maudie, and you had dealings with Lady Fairfax. These are all worrying facts."

"I've explained that, not that I should have to," Gil said.

"We can work together if you give me your alibi for the night of Cora's murder. I need to be sure I'm not working with a villain."

He chuckled. "You will be. I'm one of the best in this rotten city, but I'm not a killer. At least, I didn't murder Cora. And I'd never lay a hand on my Iris."

"Then where were you on the evening of Cora's murder?"

Gil puffed a breath, his gaze flitting around the room before resolve entered his gaze. "There was a dog race in the Medway Towns. I took the train with a friend, and we met up with some others. I was there all night. I missed the last train, so I kipped at my friend's before heading back the next day. I got an earful from Iris for that and for all the money I lost."

"Thank you. If you provide me with your friend's details, I'll speak to them. Once your alibi is confirmed, and you guarantee you won't creep into this house and attempt to stab me in my sleep again, we may investigate together."

Gil hesitated and then gave me his friend's name and a telephone number. I tucked the information away and nodded.

"Thank you." I held out my hand for a shake. "Now, it's time for you to leave."

"A word to the wise," Gil said as he paused by my bedroom door. "Improve your back door security. And get a better attack dog."

I inhaled sharply. "You didn't hurt Felix, did you?"

"That soppy dog? He took one look at me, rolled over, and demanded a belly rub. I know you have a vicious dog, so I came prepared, but I didn't see him."

"Benji was injured protecting me at Iris's salon," I said. "Where is Felix?"

"Probably finishing the sausages I brought with me. It's the easiest way to calm any dog," Gil said. "Get a dog that'll actually bite an intruder. You'll be much safer."

"This is a safe neighbourhood," I said. "It's only you dragging down its reputation."

He chuckled. "Then I'd best be off, hadn't I?"

I sank onto the bed, watching as the door closed quietly behind Gil. Despite not revealing how he and Iris planned to make money from Cora, I had a good idea.

Cora had been smart, and no doubt Genevieve was, too. They kept records of their clientele. And if those records came to light, it would cause the scandal of the decade.

Blackmail was a nasty business, but profitable for those who were successful. Gil wanted that information to line his pockets so he could give Iris her dream of travelling. That was why he wanted access to

Cora's belongings and had confronted Genevieve in the brothel.

This was the reason those murders happened. But before I could get the police to believe it, I needed proof.

Chapter 18

"Did you have a visitor last night?" My mother tucked into the poached eggs Matthew had made her. I perched on the end of her bed, enjoying a bowl of porridge. Matthew sat on the other side, trying to stop Felix from eating most of his breakfast.

"I returned home alone," I said. "Why do you ask?"

"I heard you talking. You weren't talking to yourself, were you?"

"How did you hear me, since your bedroom is downstairs?" I'd been worried my mother or Matthew might have overheard the commotion from the night before.

"I was shuffling to the kitchen to get a glass of milk. I called several times for one of you to help me, but as usual, I was ignored," my mother said.

"We never ignore you," I said. "And you're perfectly capable of pouring a glass of milk."

"I wondered why the milk was going down so quickly," Matthew said. "I can always make you a milky drink before you go to sleep."

"I don't want you to go to any trouble on my account," she said.

Matthew caught my eye and arched a brow.

My mother continued, "It was when I was coming back from the kitchen that I heard your sister chatting away."

"I must have been talking in my sleep," I said.

"You've never talked in your sleep before," my mother persisted. "You didn't sneak Jacob in, did you? I understand you are close, but leave that sort of thing until you're married."

"Jacob is happily down in Kent, working on a wonderfully complex fraud case that has seized his interest. I snuck no one into my room last night." And that was the truth. Gil had broken in. Which reminded me, I needed to secure the services of a locksmith for our back door.

My mother glared at me with narrowed eyes, not convinced by my explanation.

"The case is progressing," I added, hoping a change of topic would distract her. "Although the police refuse to let Maudie go, I'm confident I'll get her free any day now."

"Who do you like for the murders?" Matthew asked.

"I thought it was a local criminal. One I've seen in the Rusty Nail but also lurking around Belgravia."

"What were you doing in Belgravia?" my mother exclaimed.

"Following clues." I decided not to tell her I'd been inside a brothel for fear the heart palpitations would go on for a week.

"You must be careful pursuing criminals," my mother said. "Especially if this one killed those poor women."

"He didn't. And he surprised me. He could be useful," I said. "It turns out he had an attachment to one of the victims, and he wants justice for her."

"You can't work with a criminal!" my mother said. "It'll tarnish your reputation."

"I'm happy to work with him if it helps me to figure out what happened," I said. "The police are doing nothing, as usual. Detective Chief Inspector Taylor is fixated on Maudie and wants to solve the case fast, regardless of whether he has the right person. It's a short-sighted way to conduct business. Leave the criminals on the streets, and they'll continue to stir trouble."

"Don't neglect your proper work," my mother said. "I had Harry on the telephone yesterday, concerned about you."

"Not concerned about my work, surely," I said. "I've yet to miss a deadline, and I don't intend to."

"He's concerned you're overtaxing yourself," my mother said. "I'm worried about that, too. You're neglecting everyone, including us. I barely see you."

"I'm here now, and we're enjoying breakfast together," I said. "Sometimes I must occupy myself with other things. We must clear up these murders, or the Rusty Nail's reputation will decay. That would be bad for business."

My mother flapped her hand in the air. "After this case, it's time you retired. Jacob will propose any day now, so that should be your focus."

Matthew chuckled. "Can you imagine Veronica as a bored housewife? She wouldn't be happy spending her days dusting the ornaments and ironing Jacob's shirts."

The very thought sent shivers down my spine. I finished my porridge and stood. "I must get to work. I have a busy day."

"Don't get yourself into any more trouble," my mother said. "And you'll change your mind once Jacob proposes. A woman always does when she realises how important marriage is."

"Are you sure you're my mother?" I stopped at the bedroom door. "You raised me to think differently."

"I did no such thing. That was all your father's doing. I blame him for your foolhardy shenanigans."

Matthew took my empty bowl. "Escape while you can. It sounds like she's about to go on one of her rants."

I kissed his cheek. "You're an angel. I'll see you tonight, Mother." I dashed out, put on my shoes, grabbed my handbag, and then hurried to work.

I barely raised my head all morning, determined to complete my tasks, because I needed a couple of hours in the afternoon to undertake some investigations.

Once I was finished, I popped into Uncle Harry's office. "Do you know of a centre or charity that helps fallen women?"

His brow wrinkled, and he stared off into space. "Churches usually help with such a thing. Why do you want to know?"

"I need to speak to any women who worked at the Belgravia brothel Cora ran," I said. "I think she kept records about her clients and was killed because she misused that information."

Uncle Harry's eyes lit up at the potential for a story, and he whistled. "Blackmail! It's a possibility, but you'll need proof."

"Which is why I need to find some of Cora's girls and get them talking."

"Take money, cigarettes, and gin," Uncle Harry said.

"It sounds like you have experience in such matters." I arched an eyebrow.

He chuckled. "It always pays to know how to get someone to open up."

"Do you know who runs these centres?"

"Father Kersey is a prominent figure in that work. I met him once at a public event. He's a pious sort, but his heart is in the right place."

"I know him! He frequents the Rusty Nail, and he visited Maudie at the police station." That was handy. Since we already had a connection, he might allow me access to the women.

"You could see if he has a weakness for gin or cigarettes, too." Uncle Harry laughed. "Or maybe it should be ale. I remember he enjoyed a few pints when we spoke."

"Perhaps a donation to the cause would make him more helpful," I said. "These places never have enough money. And I could volunteer a few hours of my time."

"If anyone can sway a man of the cloth, it's you. I'd wish you good luck, but I doubt you'll need it," Uncle Harry said.

"I do need a few hours off, but all my tasks are done," I said.

"Off you go. Investigate, but tell me what you find out. This has the makings of an excellent story."

I made a quick telephone call to the police station and was fortunate to get through to Sergeant Matthers. He put Maudie on the line, who confirmed that the Church of All Saints, a few streets over from the Rusty Nail, was where Father Kersey ran his centre.

I hurried over, stopping at a nearby bank to withdraw some funds and then make a few essential purchases, and then hastened to the church. It was a solid, practical structure typical of Tudor-era parish churches. Made of local pale stone, with a square tower and simple arched windows.

Several women were going inside as I drew closer, and when I stepped in, the place was a hive of activity.

The women who'd entered before me walked straight through the church and turned left, so I followed. There was a large room at the back with several doors leading off it. Temporary beds lined either side of the room, and teacups, jugs of water, platters of sandwiches, and fruit covered a table. Several older women bustled about, arranging things, while smaller groups of younger women sat together, engaged in various tasks.

"May I help you?" An older woman bustled over. "Are you here for reading classes? Or we have a health and education programme beginning in twenty minutes."

"Thank you. I'm not here for the classes. Is Father Kersey available? I'd like to donate to his worthy cause."

"Oh, how wonderful! Does he know you're visiting?"

"No, but we're acquainted. I'm sure he won't mind a brief visit."

"Right this way. He'll be delighted to receive your donation." She bustled me along. "We never have enough of anything, and we get more and more ladies coming in every month, seeking help. We do what we can, but it never feels like enough."

"It seems you do excellent work."

"God always finds a way." She knocked briskly on a door and opened it to reveal Father Kersey, sitting behind a large desk surrounded by papers.

I stepped inside and shook his hand before reminding him of our connection. "I hope you don't mind the intrusion, but when I heard of your first-rate work, I had to come along. This is my donation to your venture."

Father Kersey looked inside the envelope I handed him, and his eyes widened. "My dear lady, this is marvellous."

"It comes with one or two strings. Nothing onerous, but I'd like to talk to some ladies who use your service and see how they're faring. Learn if there's anything extra they need. This doesn't need to be a singular donation. I'm always looking for worthy causes to support."

Father Kersey secured the money in a desk drawer. "The women aren't always forthcoming, but there are several who may talk to you. The older ones like to gossip. While I find someone suitable, I'll get Doris to show you around."

I thanked him and spent the next fifteen minutes visiting small classrooms, a space where the women could wash their clothes and have a bath, and the food preparation area.

By the time I returned to the main room, the Bible study was already underway. There weren't many women there, and those who were didn't seem all that impressed and focussed on the tea and biscuits.

Father Kersey beckoned me over, and I thanked Doris for her time before joining him. He sat with two women in their late thirties. One of them smiled at me, revealing only a few teeth, and the other looked utterly beaten down, her shoulders sagging.

"This is Mary and Julie," Father Kersey said. "They've been coming to the church for two years and are loyal helpers. You ladies also like a good chat, don't you?"

"For the right price," Mary muttered, her attention on me. "You another do-gooder come to save our souls, are you?"

"Thank you, Father Kersey," I said. "Would you mind if I spoke to these ladies alone?"

He looked a trifle concerned, but Doris called him over when another priest entered the church. "I'm sure a few minutes will be fine. I won't be long," he said, hurrying away.

Julie rolled her eyes. "The silly old fool wanted to drag us to Bible studies. Then he said if we didn't do that, we had to talk to you. I suppose it beats cleaning up his mess, though. Who knew a priest could be so untidy?"

Mary huffed an agreement. "Free help. That's how he sees us. He's always sending us off to clean and heft boxes and the like. The last job I did for him almost put my back out! He only uses us because he's too cheap to hire a professional."

"I suppose it's good to stay busy," I said. "And I hope to be more entertaining than Bible studies."

Julie snorted. "What do you want to talk to us about?"

"I'm investigating what happened to Cora Bellamy and Iris Dane," I said. "Did you know those ladies?"

That got their attention, and they sat up straighter.

"Everyone knew Cora," Mary said. "What's it to you?"

"Planning on starting your own brothel, are you?" Julie cackled. "You don't seem the type."

"I own the Rusty Nail where Cora's body was found," I replied. "I'd like to know who had the nerve to poison her in my establishment."

"Crikey, that's a turn-up for the books," Mary said. "I lost touch with Cora after I left the brothel. It was getting too much for me. These bodies wear out quickly if they're overused, if you get my meaning."

Julie stood and made a lewd gesture with her hips.

"Do either of you know if Cora kept records of her clients?" I asked.

"What's with all the snooping?" Julie asked.

"We want no trouble. Cora treated us right," Mary added. "She worked us hard, but the pay was good, and she looked out for us if we had health problems. I don't want you bad-mouthing her."

"I promise you I won't." I extracted a packet of cigarettes from my handbag. "Do either of you ladies smoke?"

They grabbed at the cigarettes. Julie got to them first. I took out another packet. "There's plenty to go around. And how about a drink?"

"We can't. Not in here," Mary said. "Father Kersey doesn't like it. He says drink corrupts the soul."

"We're already corrupted. Souls as dark as the night." Julie chortled as she lit up.

"What about some chocolate?" I asked.

The women's eyes widened as I pulled out a large bar of Bournville, opened it, and shared it between us.

"I liked Iris," Mary said, chewing thoughtfully. "I was sad to hear what happened to her. I thought she'd got out of that business, cleaned herself up. But from what I've heard, she was still operating a back-room service."

"I can confirm she was," I said. "I visited recently and had my hair cut by Iris."

Julie shook her head. "She'd never cut your hair so wonky. Iris was talented. She even did me a time or two. Made me look ever so fancy."

"We had a disagreement, and she refused to finish the job," I said. "The wonky side is my doing."

Julie laughed. "That sounds like Iris. It's so unfair what happened to her."

"Can you think of anyone who would want either lady dead?"

Mary and Julie exchanged a look and shrugged.

"Do you know anything about the records Cora kept about her gentlemen?" I asked.

"Maybe we do. Maybe we don't. What else you got in that handbag?" Julie asked.

I handed over another bar of chocolate and the last packet of cigarettes. "Did Cora use her client records for financial gain?"

"Blackmail, you mean?" Mary asked.

"Cora selected a specific clientele for her brothel," I said. "Men of influence. That information has value."

Mary leant closer. "Cora made us tell her what our clients liked. She wanted all the details, no matter how… unnatural. She'd write it down in these journals she kept."

"She never said what she used that information for," Julie continued the story. "But even those of us who aren't all that clever knew what she was up to. She'd get this look in her eye when she got something big. Next thing you knew, she'd be in a new fur coat, or flashing diamonds, or a wad of cash."

"That's how she got so rich, so fast?" I said more to myself than to the ladies. And it was what got her killed. She'd served powerful men, and they demanded discretion. If she'd pressed a client too hard, it was no surprise they'd silenced her. "Can you think of any clients she may have pushed too far?"

"We've been out of that game too long to know for certain. The men come and go," Julie replied. "Could've been one of a dozen. Or someone new she took on."

"What about the records?" I asked. "Did Cora pass them on to Iris? Was that why she was targeted?"

Mary shrugged again. "It's possible. They were close. Iris learnt everything she knew from Cora. She took her under her wing because she saw something in her."

"Do you know where Cora kept the records of her gentlemen?"

"She had a private office at the club," Mary said. "The new madam may have them, or one of the girls might've taken them."

"I reckon they could still be there, you know," Julie said. "One night, I saw Cora put something behind a false panel in the wall. Never got a look inside, but I figured it was a safe or somewhere she kept her jewels. If I were poking around for those journals, that's where I'd look."

"Thank you, ladies." I snuck them the bottle of gin and pressed a finger to my lips. "Don't let Father Kersey see that."

As if summoned by mentioning his name, he hurried towards us, his hands clasped together.

"My apologies for leaving you on your own. Mary, Julie, I encourage you to join Bible studies. You know how important it is to spend time with our good Lord. He must see how repentant you are."

The women had magically hidden the contraband I'd given them. They muttered something unintelligible and shuffled off, their heads bowed.

Father Kersey watched them go then turned to me. "And how about you, Miss Vale? Do you have time for our Lord? He welcomes all, no matter how late they are in finding him."

I made a show of checking my watch. "Good gracious, I must dash. I've so much to do."

He sighed. "That's a pity. God sees all."

"Then perhaps he could answer the mystery of what happened to Cora and Iris." I rose and collected my considerably lighter handbag.

Father Kersey's cheeks flushed. "We have free will, which means bad things happen. He cannot prevent that. The one who committed those crimes will be punished. If not on this earth, then at Heaven's gates."

"That's something I'm not prepared to wait for. Good afternoon, Father." I hurried out of the church. I had to get those journals. But the only way to do that was to break into the Belgravia brothel. And from what I'd seen during my visit, security there was tight.

I needed help from someone who was unbothered about breaking the rules or a few locks. Perhaps even a skull or two. And I knew just the chap for the job.

Chapter 19

It had just gone half-past two in the morning as I stood in the shadows opposite the Belgravia brothel. I pulled up the collar of my thick, warm woollen coat and shoved my hands deep into the pockets to keep warm.

Footsteps approached, and a few seconds later, Gil came into view. He was dressed equally warmly, with a hat pulled low over his brow. He joined me in the shadows and grunted a greeting.

"The place should have closed by now, shouldn't it?" I murmured.

"These places keep the hours they like," he replied. "It should shut any minute. We'll need to wait a bit for the staff to clear out. There are always a few who stay to tidy. They do the main cleaning in the morning, though, so they won't be long."

"Are you sure nobody stays on-site overnight for security?"

"I figured everyone would clear out, but once we're inside, we'll know for sure," Gil said.

"I appreciate the assistance. I usually have helpers, but they're indisposed."

"What happened to them?" Gil asked. "Got locked up, did they?"

"Benji has an injured foot. Jacob is busy in Kent. And my friend Ruby is... well, let's say she's undertaking a long-term mission that will take the rest of her life to complete."

He slid me a curious look. "Interesting company you keep. Who's Jacob?"

"My partner. He helps run our private investigation firm in Kent."

We fell silent as several people hurried out of the club. They were all girls, so it seemed likely there were no clients left inside. Gil slid a small flask from his pocket and took a sip before offering it to me.

"I'd rather have a clear head," I said.

"It'll keep the chill off."

"Thank you, but no."

"Suit yourself." Gil took another swig then pocketed the flask.

Two more girls left, hurrying away.

We waited another ten minutes in silence.

Several security men emerged, smoking cigarettes and talking quietly. They strolled away along the empty street.

"I reckon that's it," Gil said. "We'll go around the back. The locks on all the doors are good, but I can jimmy our way in."

I checked both sides of the street to ensure no one was watching, then we hurried across the road and down the alleyway beside the brothel. Gil led the way, as he knew the building's layout better than I did.

He stopped at a door and tested the handle. "It's locked tight. This'll take me a few minutes. You watch to make sure no one notices us." Gil crouched and inspected the lock.

I walked back along the alley and peered out. Given the late hour, there was no one about, not even a stray dog or a rat looking for scraps. Soft curses and complaints drifted along the alley, accompanied by the faint sound of metal grinding.

I kept watch while Gil worked on the lock. Though I wasn't entirely comfortable working with him, given his criminal inclinations, I knew he wouldn't hesitate to help me gain entry to the brothel. I'd been candid with him about what I was looking for, and he'd agreed so long as he could take anything else of value we found.

Theft wasn't something I approved of, but Gil had the skills I needed and the lack of scruples to complete the task. And although I'd also technically be stealing the journals, I was doing it for the greater good, as Father Kersey would no doubt say.

There was a quiet clatter behind me, and I turned to see Gil standing with the door open. I hurried back along the alley.

"This way to the office," he muttered.

I grabbed his arm and pulled him back. "Wait! I heard a noise. There's someone still in here."

Gil shrugged off my hand. "I'll deal with them. That's what you brought me here for, isn't it?"

I hesitated. I hadn't only wanted Gil here because he knew his way around a lock. He was swift with his fists and disturbingly efficient. "Don't kill them. Just make sure they're out of action long enough for us to find what we need."

"I'll make no promises." He strode into the darkness.

A few seconds later, there was a loud shout, followed by a crash.

Whilst Gil was occupied, I hurried around the edge of the room, trying doors in search of the office. It took me a moment, but I soon discovered what I was looking for. I was about to enter when a solid hand landed on my shoulder.

"You're not one of Genevieve's girls."

I whirled around and came face to face with a broad chest. I tipped my head back to look at a scowling brute of a man, the potent smell of whisky on his breath.

"I'm a new recruit," I blurted out. "I had a few questions for Genevieve. Is she still here?"

He stepped back, his gaze sweeping over my practical shoes, sensible trousers, and thick woollen coat. "I know some men have peculiar tastes, but I'm not sure what look you're going for. Sensible schoolteacher?"

"I was trying for head librarian," I said coolly.

His gaze narrowed. "Genevieve introduces all the girls to us, so we know who to protect. I've never met you."

"Then you're clearly terrible at your job," I said. "Is Genevieve here or not?"

"If you were one of her girls, you'd know her hours. She never stays until the end. We're left to supervise and make sure the girls get out safely. Why are you really here?"

There was another crash behind us. The chap who'd accosted me glanced away to see what was going on. That was the opportunity I needed.

I moved fast. A sharp jab to the throat stunned him long enough for me to duck beneath his grasp and drive my knee into his stomach. He doubled over with a grunt, but he was thickset and quick to recover. He swung at me, a heavy-handed blow I barely dodged, feeling the air stir past my cheek.

I spun to the side, seized a lamp from the nearby table, and smashed it across his shoulder. The glass shattered, sending him stumbling. He regained his footing, snarling now, his face flushed with rage. He lunged.

This time, I let him come. At the last second, I stepped aside, hooked my foot behind his, and sent him sprawling with a thud. Before he could rise, I pressed a foot against his chest and brought my elbow down hard across the side of his head.

He went still.

I stood, breath ragged, hand throbbing where the shattered glass had nicked me. Not too bad, and nothing that would stop me.

Gil reappeared, holding his ribs and panting. "I saw what you did. That was impressive."

"Likewise. Your poor fellow's still breathing, isn't he?" I asked, touching a sore spot on my arm that would bloom into a glorious bruise.

"He'll live. He didn't go down easy, though." Gil drew himself upright, though he kept one arm wrapped around his middle. "Are you taken?"

"Taken as in..."

"Do you have a fancy man?"

"Why do you want to know?" I asked.

"You remind me of Iris. She had fire in her veins, and she could fight like an alley cat."

"You're not suggesting..." I waved a finger in the air between us.

He raised one shoulder. "I need a woman who can stand up for herself. Someone who can work beside me. I can't abide shrinking violets who whimper at the first sign of trouble. You don't do that."

"I appreciate the compliment," I said. "But I'm very much taken and happily so. The partner I mentioned, Jacob, we aren't just business partners."

"If you ever have a change of heart, you know where I am."

"I'll bear it in mind. Let's get searching, shall we?"

Gil opened the door and gestured for me to step through first.

The office contained a large desk, several filing cabinets, a bookshelf, and various drawers. Rather than rummage through them, I tapped along the wall, listening for a hollow sound. Gil, meanwhile, made a thorough search of the desk. He pocketed several items, which I pretended not to see. If I didn't know about his crimes, I couldn't report him.

After several minutes of tapping, I found a panel that sounded different from the rest. It was near the floor, tucked beside the bookshelf.

"Have you got something?" Gil joined me.

I pressed against the panel. One corner gave. I wriggled it free and peered inside. There were three leather-bound journals, several piles of cash, and a small box. When I opened the box, it revealed a variety of rings and earrings, each set with precious stones.

"Is this what you're looking for?" Gil was already grabbing the cash and stuffing it into his pockets.

"You shouldn't take all of it," I said.

"We made a deal. You find those journals, and I keep anything else I fancy."

"That's an awful lot of money."

"I'll make a donation to a good cause."

"The Gil Renwick Cause?"

He grunted a laugh. "I might just do that."

"I know an excellent animal shelter in Battersea. I'll turn a blind eye if you donate to them."

He paused. "How much?"

"At least one bundle of money. You can keep all the jewels."

"I'll consider it."

"You'll do it." I held out my hand to shake on the agreement.

Gil scowled at me. "You're a tough nut."

"It is a remarkable place. You won't regret helping the animals."

"I regret ever meeting you." Gil grabbed my hand and shook. "What do those journals say?"

I moved to the window, where the full moon offered just enough light to read. The journals were written up in date order. Each page listed names and had sums of money beside them, along with women's names, most likely the gentlemen's preferred lady.

I whistled under my breath. "My word. Some of these men spend extraordinary sums here."

"Cora catered to all tastes. I've heard there were strange requests, things most places won't accommodate. The men got to do as they desired so long as the girls weren't hurt. At least that's what Iris said."

I flicked through several pages. There were so many influential names that I wasn't sure where to begin. If Cora threatened to reveal they'd used her services, they'd be ruined. And they were all powerful enough to want her silenced.

"You find the right blinder," Gil said. "I don't care how powerful he is. He could sit on the throne, and I'd still do him in."

"I appreciate your passion, but we need hard evidence to prove which gentleman was behind these crimes."

"I can work through the list. These days, there are too many snobs taking all the money."

"That's taking things rather too far," I said.

"Give me those journals," Gil said. "Maybe I'll see a name I know that caused a scuffle."

I held them tight. "I want to check each page carefully and find a connection between one of these gentlemen, Cora, and Iris. If our killer favoured these ladies, he may have also shared his darkest secrets with them, which were then used to blackmail him, without realising how dangerous he was."

"You should still give those journals to me." Gil held out his hand.

"So you may continue the blackmail?" I glanced at his bulging pockets. "You've got more than enough from this deal."

"Hand them over." He met my gaze.

I stared right back at him. "Don't tell me you're a man who goes back on his word. Aren't you doing this for Iris? Or has greed got the better of you?"

He smiled slightly and raised a hand, but suddenly froze, his head whipping towards the door. "There's someone out there."

I tucked the journals into my bag and fastened it then crept after Gil. We peered into the club's gloomy interior.

"I don't see anyone," I whispered. "The chaps we dealt with are still out cold. Could it be a girl?"

"No, someone always sees them off the premises before locking the doors." Gil looked around slowly.

"We've got what we came for," I murmured. "Let's go."

Gil huffed out a breath then nodded and led the way to the exit. We slipped outside, and he secured the door behind us before we hurried along the alleyway.

We were just walking away when I grabbed Gil's arm. "Over there! Someone's watching us from the shadows. Do you see?"

Gil's hands fisted, and he glared at the spot I pointed to. "I don't see anyone."

I blinked. Whoever was there had vanished. "I'm certain someone was standing there. I saw them move. The same thing happened at the Rusty Nail. Just after I found Cora's body, I looked out the window, and someone was watching the pub. Benji gave chase, but they got away."

"You're jumpy." Gil grinned at me. "Is this your first break in?"

"I choose not to answer that. And it's no surprise my nerves are a touch frazzled," I said. "After your late-night visit, I'll be sleeping with one eye open tonight."

"You could always sleep with me, you know. For protection, like."

I chuckled. "Thank you, but I know very well how to look after myself."

"Having seen you in action, I believe it," Gil said. "Let me walk you to your car. That way, no shadowy figures can accost you. But if they do, they'll have to deal with my fists."

"They'd be dealing with mine too," I said. "Thank you. I appreciate the offer."

We walked along in silence.

"I'll review the journal entries and see what connections I can make," I said.

"Don't hold out on me, Veronica," Gil said. "I'll know if you're lying."

"Whyever would I do that?"

"Because you want whoever killed Iris and Cora behind bars. Whereas I want to see them six feet under. They deserve nothing less after what they did."

"We both believe in justice. We just administer it through different means," I said. "I'll keep you informed, but not so you can commit murder."

"I could take those journals from you, you know," Gil said.

"But you have honour. And we're partners now. You wouldn't double-cross your new partner, would you?" I stopped by my car, which I'd parked several streets away from the brothel, and turned to Gil, fully prepared to fight him if I had to.

He stared down at me then sighed and looked away. "If you didn't remind me so much of Iris, I would. You take care. I'll be in touch."

I whispered good night, slid into my car, and shut the door. I blew out a breath and sat back in my seat. Now

I had the evidence, I just needed to pick through it and find whatever connected Cora, Iris, and the killer.

Chapter 20

I went to open the back door of the Rolls Royce, but Lady M's most efficient chauffeur had already hurried around and set to the task.

After offering him a word of thanks, I strode towards the entrance of Lady M's grand home. She'd summoned me early to take breakfast with her and Ruby. Although I had a hundred and one tasks to attend to, not least of which was unmasking a killer, it was never wise to refuse Lady M. And I'd promised I'd take better care of my friendship with Ruby.

I also missed Benji, so it was no great hardship to set aside an hour and join them.

The butler escorted me into Ruby's parlour, as I'd taken to calling it. Tea was just being poured by one of Lady M's household staff. Ruby was sitting up, wearing a voluminous pale blue dress, which unfortunately highlighted the dark circles beneath her pretty eyes.

Benji climbed off the chaise longue they'd been lounging on and hurried over to greet me. I spent a few moments patting him and checking his injury, glad to see him on the mend.

"If only you greeted me so warmly," Ruby said with a touch of tartness.

"You're next on the list. Should I scratch behind your ears or pat your belly?" I stood and brushed Benji's fur from my hands. "Did you both sleep well?"

"Benji was restless. He's missing you," Ruby said. "And he keeps looking out the window."

"He knows I'll come back for him. You're looking after each other." I noticed Ruby said nothing about how well she'd slept, but her appearance told me everything. "How are you feeling?"

She wrinkled her nose. "As if you can't tell. I feel thoroughly uncomfortable. I was restless all night, too."

"Is there something on your mind, or is it a physical ailment?" I settled into a seat and selected a cup of tea.

"My lower back aches. No matter what position I get into, the discomfort won't abate."

"Has Lady M summoned the doctor?"

"It's not the first time this has happened. He told me to apply a warm compress and find a more comfortable position. Honestly, men do not know the trials women endure when with child."

"It's a pity there aren't more female doctors." I sipped my tea. "I have something to take your mind off your aches and pains. I went out last night with an accomplice and uncovered information about the murders."

Ruby's forehead furrowed. "An accomplice? Have you replaced me?"

"Heavens forbid! And this isn't the sort of accomplice I care to deal with regularly. In fact, until recently, he was a suspect in the investigation."

"What have you been getting yourself into this time, Veronica?" Lady M swept into the parlour, and right behind her came the servers, who presented us with crumpets, toast, poached eggs, bacon, and every manner of breakfast delight one could imagine.

"I went hunting for evidence," I said and took a moment to recount to Ruby and Lady M my late-night adventures at the Belgravia brothel.

"You took a risk." Ruby nibbled on an unbuttered crumpet. "What if Gil is behind all of this? He might have knocked you over the head then stolen the jewels, the money, and the journals."

"As you can see, I'm still standing," I said. "Gil was helpful. I believe he genuinely cared for Iris. When he learned of her murder, he was overcome with grief."

"Men can be deceitful creatures," Lady M said. "Perhaps he's pulling the wool over your eyes."

"He provided me with an alibi for the night of Cora's murder," I said. "I had to ring the telephone number several times this morning before anyone answered, but they confirmed Gil was in another county when Cora died."

Ruby squirmed in her seat and rubbed her lower back.

Lady M was instantly on the alert. "What do you need, my girl? Another warm compress?" She was already summoning a member of the household staff to attend to it.

"If you wouldn't mind," Ruby said. "Perhaps I should walk. It may shift things around a bit."

"I'll have Annie escort you outside, but just a gentle stroll. You don't want to exert yourself." Lady M had everything sorted in under a minute, and Ruby was soon shuffling out through the open French doors leading onto the garden with an attentive maid by her side.

"Don't talk about anything exciting while I'm gone," Ruby called over her shoulder.

I finished my first crumpet, waiting until Ruby was out of earshot before turning to Lady M. "Perhaps she should go to a hospital or a maternity unit. I don't like how pale she looks."

"She refuses to leave," Lady M said. "I'm paying for the doctor to come daily so nothing is missed. I always thought Ruby was robust, but this child has taken it out of her."

"You are marvellous for opening your house to her," I said.

"Oh, what nonsense," Lady M replied. "I rarely tell her, but she's my favourite employee. I never had a daughter, but I like to think that if I'd had one, she'd be like Ruby. Well, perhaps not get herself into such a muddle as this. But she's full of spirit. She brings every room to life and is always laughing, although not so much recently. But once this baby is born, things will return to normal."

My gaze rested on the open door. "I hope so. Although she'll be a mother, so her life will alter."

"Not as much as you might think," Lady M said. "We've interviewed excellent nannies and a wet nurse, should Ruby desire one. She will be free to return to work or to gallivant about with you on hare-brained missions whenever she so wishes. A child shouldn't hold a woman back."

"Not all women have access to such vast resources," I said.

Lady M tilted her head in acknowledgement. "A reasonable statement. But since I have the resources, I intend to use them. I consider Ruby part of my family. Therefore, she has access to my money, and I shall insist she uses it. Fear not. You haven't lost Ruby. She will return to adventuring soon enough."

A warm ball of happiness settled in my stomach at the thought life might return to normal. I'd desperately missed having Ruby by my side. It had been a strange investigation thus far, forsaking Ruby and Benji and teaming up with a hardened criminal. I never liked change at the best of times, but this had been a step too far.

I'd just finished another delicious, buttered crumpet when Ruby shuffled back into the room, a faint pink glow on her cheeks. "That's better. Although I'm waddling like a duck! I'm glad there was nobody out there to see me."

"You make a beautiful duck," Lady M said with a smile.

"Now we're all here," I said, "let's look through the journals. There are three of them, so we've one each to explore."

Ruby grasped the leather-bound journal I offered and began reading. Lady M perched a pair of spectacles on the end of her nose and examined hers. I'd already looked through the one in my hands, but I flicked through the pages again.

"My word," Lady M exclaimed. "I recognise these names. If this information were to get out, there would be societal ruin. And many of these so-called gentlemen are married with families. Shame on them."

Ruby had her nose buried in the journal. "There are several lords. I've even spotted a viscount."

"Cora catered to the highest levels of society," I said. "She charged a pretty penny, but must have wanted more. From the vast amount of money and jewels concealed in that hidden panel, she'd been blackmailing many men."

"And you believe that's what got her killed?" Lady M looked up from the journal.

"It's an obvious motive," I said.

"Who do you still have as a suspect for these crimes?" Lady M asked.

"My landlady, Maudie, is still the police's chief suspect," I said. "And it's true she has no alibi, but there's also no motive. Maudie has been dishonest, but I don't believe it was her."

"What about this criminal type you've been dealing with?" Lady M enquired.

"Gilbert Renwick has the record to fit the crimes, and he uses a blade as his weapon of choice. But the news of Iris's murder devastated him."

"The man could have a vicious temper. He lashed out at his beloved then tried to cover it up," Lady M said.

"It's possible. But he was genuine when speaking about their relationship, and he has an alibi for Cora's murder. I also have another puzzle," I murmured. "Who took Iris's body?"

"If you find the body, you find the killer," Ruby said.

"Or killers. Iris was small, so perhaps a strong chap moved her on his own, but it would have been difficult in such a short time frame."

"Could Iris have murdered Cora?" Ruby asked. "Someone retaliated?"

"I pondered that possibility," I said. "But how will I ever learn that truth, now Iris is dead?"

"I thought Lady Fairfax most unhelpful when she was here," Lady M remarked. "Do you still consider her a suspect?"

"She could have paid someone to commit the crimes," I replied. "Her son is still deeply involved in the brothel, and Lady Fairfax despises that. She's desperate to preserve the family's reputation, while Tarquin seems determined to ruin it."

"If I were her," Ruby said, "I'd get rid of the son, rather than the ladies he associates with."

"Lady Fairfax would never believe her son was the problem," Lady M said with a sniff. "It's always the women who are the issue. Cunning, manipulative, leading her innocent boy astray and corrupting him with their wayward charms."

"How unfairly typical," I said. "I also considered Camille Hartley. She's a local journalist, desperate for a story."

"Would she be desperate enough to commit a double murder to get it?" Ruby asked.

"She's a woman in journalism," I said. "And she lied about the real reason she was so interested in Cora, although she was quick enough to share information when she realised how serious things had become."

"You still have a full list of suspects on your hands," Lady M observed. "And let's not forget you were at the Rusty Nail on the night of the murder. Perhaps it was you."

Ruby chuckled. "Poison is too delicate for Veronica. A blade! Now you're talking. Sharp as her tongue."

I smiled. "That would be my weapon of choice. Although perhaps a gun. Less messy, and you don't have to get so close."

"You girls are dreadful," Lady M declared with mock horror.

"If Detective Chief Inspector Taylor had his way, he'd see me charged with both crimes, just to be rid of me," I said. "Put away for life. Perhaps even hanged."

"Any man who is shown up by a woman will be full of hatred," Lady M said. "They must be the cleverest creatures in the room, or else the world is ending. We can't have the natural order spinning off its axis and us showing them up now, can we?"

Ruby turned a page in the journal she'd been studying. Her eyes widened, and she gasped.

"Have you found something?" I leant over to peer at the page she was reading. "Oh, my!"

"From the twinkle in your eye, I can tell you've solved this mystery," Lady M said.

"I believe I have," I replied. "But to bring the killer to justice, I'll once again require your assistance."

Chapter 21

"You still haven't told me why you got such a ghastly haircut?" Ruby had fussed with my hair for ten minutes ever since I'd arrived back at Lady M's for an impromptu dinner that evening.

"It was in the name of justice," I said. "And it's not that bad, is it?"

"The style is too fashionable for you." Ruby curled a strand of my hair around one finger.

"Are you suggesting I'm unfashionable?"

She chortled. "You're the height of practicality, which makes sense, given all the running about you do. Not to worry. It will soon grow out. I've trimmed the uneven side." Ruby stepped back, her gaze running over me. "You'll do."

"I should hope I will. I smell like a florist, and my face feels sticky with whatever concoction you've rubbed into my skin."

"I was primping you because I can't attend this party, thanks to that irritating Detective Chief Inspector Taylor being invited." Ruby wrinkled her nose. "It's so unfair."

"We can't risk him seeing you in your condition," I said. "He knows you've never been married, since he always asks you to date him. The man is incorrigible."

"I'll have to listen in at the top of the stairs, so be sure to leave the door open. I can't miss a thing."

"I'll ensure you don't." I glanced over my shoulder as the doorbell clanged. "That'll be our first guest. It's time for the party to begin and for our killer to be unmasked."

After meeting with Lady M and Ruby that morning and discovering the startling secret in one of Cora's journals, I'd gathered the last pieces of evidence to convict our killer. It had taken most of the day and several profuse apologies to Uncle Harry because I missed work, but I had everything in place. And Lady M had been most obliging in providing her home as the setting to unmask the killer.

In fact, the prospect of such an adventure had delighted her, and she'd noted it down as one more source of gossip to tantalise her ladies at their monthly supper club.

"Wait! I have something for Benji, too." Ruby waddled to her dressing table and extracted a smart silk bow tie, which she fastened around Benji's neck. "It matches your dress."

"That won't last five minutes," I said. "Although he does look dashing."

Benji wagged his tail, happy to be back in my company and amid the adventure. His injury was much improved, and he'd soon be back on the streets, chasing criminals in no time.

Ruby sighed. "Off you go, then. Have all the fun. But speak clearly."

"I promise you'll hear everything. And once the guests leave, you can come down and we'll enjoy dinner together," I said.

"That's if Detective Chief Inspector Taylor doesn't arrest you for poking about in something that isn't your business."

"He has no leg to stand on," I replied. "I did my best to assist him, but he dug his heels in and refused to look past Maudie as a suspect. On his head be it, if he's made to look a nincompoop."

Ruby was still chuckling as I left her bedroom with Benji and descended the stairs. Lady M's butler was escorting Lady Eugenia Fairfax and Camille Hartley into the parlour, where we were having pre-dinner drinks.

Camille spotted me and slowed. "Veronica! I didn't expect you to be here. You move in interesting circles."

"I'm here for the story, just like you," I said.

She sighed. "I need something. It's all gone rather cold in the murder investigations. My editor put me on weddings yesterday. He said I made a promise I couldn't keep, so it was my fault."

"Stick with me this evening and you'll have a story to set your stall by," I said.

Her eyes glinted with hope. "I knew there was more to this evening than a new awards ceremony for police bravery. What are you up to?"

"You'll soon see. But don't take offence when your name comes up. I must do a thorough job."

"My name? Now I'm intrigued." She linked arms with me, and we walked into the parlour together.

Detective Chief Inspector Taylor was already there in his best dress uniform. Sergeant Matthers and Sergeant

Redcote accompanied him on Lady M's insistence. Sergeant Matthers smiled warmly at me and winked. I'd tipped him off on the telephone as to what I had planned.

Poor old Detective Chief Inspector Taylor hadn't a clue what was about to hit him, and I was glad he didn't because he'd have called things off, assuming it was ridiculous nonsense.

The doorbell chimed once again, and a few seconds later, the butler brought in Gilbert Renwick. He looked smart in polished shoes and a newly tailored suit with a dapper pinstripe.

The room fell silent as everyone turned to stare at him. He grunted and hunched his shoulders. I caught his eye and beckoned him over.

"This had better be worth it," he grumbled. "Although this place has a few antiques I can sneak out while I'm here."

"Don't even think about it," I muttered. "I invited you so you can learn what happened to Iris. Be on your best behaviour, or I'll make you leave."

He slid me a glare, although there was a half-smile on his face. "I reckon you would. Fair enough. I'll keep my hands to myself."

The doorbell clanged again, and the butler escorted Father Kersey into the room. He scurried in, glancing around furtively and offering a smile.

"What's he doing here?" Gil muttered to me.

"You'll soon find out," I replied. "Keep your temper in check. There are police officers here, and they won't hesitate to arrest you."

"There are only three of them. I could take them," Gil said under his breath.

"No swinging fists or stabbing anyone," I warned. "This is about justice for Iris and Cora."

Lady M swanned into the room, resplendent in dark green velvet, a diamond tiara glittering in her hair. She smiled warmly at everyone, waiting for silence.

"Welcome to you all. I'm glad you could attend my last-minute soiree. When I heard about the marvellous work of our local police force, I felt we had to commemorate it. All I've been hearing is how hard Detective Chief Inspector Taylor has worked of late."

Detective Chief Inspector Taylor puffed out his chest.

"Our policemen and women don't get the credit they deserve, so this dinner is to celebrate them. And I have a little something special for Detective Chief Inspector Taylor to ensure this is a night he never forgets."

He preened under Lady M's continued praise. The man was a pompous peacock and about as smart as one. Although that was an insult to peacocks.

"It's a great honour to receive this invitation," Detective Chief Inspector Taylor said. "Although I must say I was a little surprised."

"Nonsense," Lady M said. "You do sterling work, and you don't get nearly enough recognition. I shall put in a good word about everything you do to keep our streets safe."

He bowed his head in acknowledgement.

"Before dinner, my dear friend Veronica Vale would like your attention. She has been working on a tricky puzzle, but she's finally figured it out." Lady M gestured for me to take the floor.

I glanced at Detective Chief Inspector Taylor and caught him scowling at me. I turned my back on him. "Thank you. As I'm sure all of you are aware, there have been two troubling murders. One at my pub, the Rusty Nail, where Cora Bellamy was poisoned. The second murder happened in Soho. Iris Dane, who ran a successful hair salon among other businesses, was stabbed to death on her own premises."

Camille was scribbling down notes furiously as I spoke.

"Given that Cora died in my pub, the case greatly interested me. Especially since my landlady, Maudie Creer, is sitting in a cell because the police believe she committed Cora's murder."

"We have every reason to believe that," Detective Chief Inspector Taylor said. "I'm not sure what is going on here. I thought this was a celebratory dinner."

"If you'll be quiet, sir, everything will soon be revealed," Lady M said sharply. "Go on, Veronica."

"Thank you," I said. "Along with my innocent landlady, I was there when Cora's body was discovered. At first, it appeared to be a natural death, but it didn't take long to realise things were awry. A window was open. There was dirt on the sill. And a scrap of paper screwed up in the wastebasket suggested Cora feared for her life."

"This is all irrelevant," Detective Chief Inspector Taylor said.

I continued as if he hadn't spoken, having expected such irritating interruptions. "After Cora died, various people visited the Rusty Nail, eager to speak to Cora or gain access to her belongings. This all points to a suspicious death."

"Caused by your landlady," Detective Chief Inspector Taylor interrupted again. "All we need is her confession, and this case can be closed."

"It's not that simple," I said. "Maudie is innocent. Yes, she's made mistakes, but she's no killer."

"You're only saying that because she works for you!"

"We cannot allow the guilty party to walk free," I snapped. "The guilty party who is currently in this room."

There were several gasps, and Camille's frantic scribbling quickened.

"My initial suspicions fell on Iris Dane. She worked for Cora. For those unaware, Cora ran a successful and prestigious brothel. Iris was one of her girls, but she struck out on her own and opened a salon in Soho. When I visited the salon, I learned two things. Iris ran her own brothel out the back of the salon, and she'd recently applied for a passport. That got me wondering if she planned to flee the country because she was guilty of a heinous crime."

"That's all supposition," Detective Chief Inspector Taylor said.

"It's factual. Iris was also seen outside the Rusty Nail on the night someone poisoned Cora. But when I questioned Iris about where she was that evening, she told me she had worked late that night in Soho and hadn't had contact with Cora for months."

"You're displaying your ineptitude, Miss Vale," Detective Chief Inspector Taylor said. "Iris and Cora were murdered in different ways."

"Be quiet, sir," Lady M cut in sharply as Detective Chief Inspector Taylor opened his mouth again. "You are disturbing Veronica's flow. And I, for one, am eager to learn who among you is the killer."

Detective Chief Inspector Taylor looked down at his shoes, his expression that of a chastised schoolboy.

"With Iris dead, my attention turned to two other suspects," I said. "Gilbert Renwick was of particular interest. He has a criminal record and known connections in the same world as our victims. He was an obvious suspect, but it turns out, an innocent one."

"You can bet a pound of jellied eels and a barrel of ale I am," Gil muttered.

"He shared a close bond with Iris. Iris's murder devastated him, and he promised vengeance," I said.

That comment got everyone's attention.

"And I'll have it, too," Gil said under his breath.

"That doesn't mean the man is innocent," Detective Chief Inspector Taylor muttered. "He's got a rotten temper."

"He has a solid alibi," I said firmly. "They confirmed his whereabouts on the night of Cora's murder."

"That means nothing," Detective Chief Inspector Taylor protested. "You can't take the word of a hardened criminal."

"Are you suggesting he's the killer and not Maudie?" I asked. "Have you made a mistake?"

"I'm suggesting nothing other than that this nonsense stops now," he barked.

"It will in just a moment," I replied. "Or are you not interested in discovering who committed a double murder so close to home?"

Detective Chief Inspector Taylor grumbled to himself and looked away.

"I'll take that as permission to continue," I said. "I wondered briefly if Camille Hartley had something to do with it. She visited Cora several times under the guise of writing a fashion history piece. However, she quickly learned Cora had a much more colourful past. It was plausible that Camille planned an exposé."

Camille dropped her pencil. "You jolly well know that was never my plan. Well, not to begin with."

"You're desperate to break a major story."

"Veronica! You know I didn't do this," Camille said. "We're on the same team. Yes, I want an exclusive, but I wouldn't kill someone to make it happen."

"Although it's a motive, it is weak. But with no alibi to support your whereabouts, I had to keep you in mind."

"Keep your mind elsewhere and find the actual killer," Camille grumbled.

My gaze drifted from suspect to suspect. "Lady Eugenia Fairfax." I turned to the formidable matriarch.

"Good gracious!" Lady Fairfax twiddled with a diamond earring. "I'm on the detective's side. Pointing the finger at everyone suggests incompetence."

"The truth of the matter is," I continued, "your son is an embarrassment. He's done his utmost to ruin your reputation, to drain the family coffers, and he's been marvellously successful at it."

"All young men run wild. That means nothing," Lady Fairfax snapped.

"You've been working with Gil to track Tarquin. I suspect you also know your son's name is in Cora's journals. You needed to protect that fact to ensure the information never became public."

"I can't imagine what you're referring to," Lady Fairfax said icily, turning to Lady M. "Why are you entertaining this farce?"

"Because Veronica is smart," Lady M said. "She knows what she's doing."

"You would never get your hands dirty yourself," I went on, "but I wondered if you'd paid Gil to make the problem go away. You thought that if Cora died, she could no longer manipulate your son."

"This is outrageous!" Lady Fairfax rose from her seat. "I won't stay and listen to another word. "

Sergeant Matthers and Sergeant Redcote blocked the door, preventing her exit.

"If you wouldn't mind waiting until the end," Sergeant Matthers said.

Lady Fairfax pouted and complained for a few seconds before returning to her original spot.

Father Kersey cleared his throat. "I am sorry to interrupt this fascinating dialogue, but you mentioned a journal? What are you referring to?"

"Ah, yes," I said. "I was about to get to the journal. You see, Cora kept meticulous records of her clients. The information goes back years. All the names, dates, and favourite girls, written in ink and carefully tucked away."

The group exchanged surprised glances, some more genuine than others.

"I wonder what Cora planned to do with that information. Do you have any ideas, Father?" I asked.

His jaw wobbled. "I can't say I do, dear lady. I work with many fallen women, but neither Cora nor Iris came to my door. I would have helped them if they had."

"You claim to help these women out of a sense of religious piety. However, I believe it's related to your guilt and a desire for redemption. Wouldn't you say that's true?" I asked.

He clutched his small glass of wine. "I do the work others turn away from. It's difficult. These women are angry and uncouth. Many have health problems. They need months of re-education and improvement. It is not a task to undertake lightly."

"And yet, you undertake it with vigour," I said. "You're determined to provide a safe place for these fallen women, as you call them."

"It is God's work. Therefore, I do it," Father Kersey said.

"Or do you do it," I said, "because your name is also in Cora's journal?"

Chapter 22

"Miss Vale! You can't expect me to believe Father Kersey had anything to do with these murders," Detective Chief Inspector Taylor said. "The man is a pillar of the community. He supports women that most organisations turn away."

"Then explain why his name is in Cora's journal," I said. "Or perhaps Father Kersey would like to do so himself."

Father Kersey drew a ragged breath and pulled back his shoulders. "Before joining the priesthood, I had sinful thoughts. But I'm reformed."

"More than thoughts. You admit to using Cora's brothel?" I asked.

"I do not!" he said. "I've been a priest for years. Cora recorded my involvement with her girls because I perform their redemption ceremonies. It purifies them."

"And what exactly do your purification rituals involve?"

"A ministry to the soul," he replied stiffly.

"Does this ministry involve touching? Or asking the girls to show you what they do to their clients?"

"I dislike your insinuations." Detective Chief Inspector Taylor strode towards me. "Father Kersey is a godly man. We attend the same confessional. And you are making a mockery of justice, attempting to pin these murders on him."

"Have you checked Father Kersey's alibi for the night of the murders?" I felt the situation slipping out of my control as Detective Chief Inspector Taylor's anger grew.

"Why would I? He was never a suspect, so there was no reason to question him," Detective Chief Inspector Taylor said.

"I was home, praying, following mass," Father Kersey said.

"Midnight Mass?" I replied. "Your church is close to the Rusty Nail, which would have allowed you to slip into the pub and poison Cora."

"This ridiculous fantasy ends now," Detective Chief Inspector Taylor said. "And my apologies, Father Kersey. Had I known this evening would be such a pantomime, I would never have come, and neither would you."

Sergeant Matthers cleared his throat. "Sorry, sir. But I looked into Father Kersey's background."

"Whyever would you waste your time doing that? I'll dock your wages for not following orders!"

Sergeant Matthers stood firm, although his face paled. "Miss Vale suggested it. She said she had her suspicions about him after speaking to some of the ladies who used his services."

"Father Kersey was at the Rusty Nail on the night of the murder," I said.

Detective Chief Inspector Taylor focussed his ire on Sergeant Matthers. "You're heading for a demotion if you keep talking."

Sergeant Matthers gulped but bravely pressed on. "Before Father Kersey became a priest, he received a caution in his hometown of Cardiff, in Wales, for bothering ladies selling their services on the streets."

"That was a misunderstanding! I wanted to redeem their lost souls," Father Kersey blustered out. "I had a strong calling to the priesthood for a long time. Before I took my vows, I saw how desperate those women were, and I wanted to help. But they wouldn't listen. They were suspicious. It was the reason I followed this path and became a priest. Everyone trusts a priest."

"Perhaps they shouldn't," I said. "It seems you're repeating your sins. Cora confronted you, and you grew nervous that she'd ruin your reputation."

"I was unaware Cora had recorded my redemption ceremonies, but it is nothing I'm ashamed of," Father Kersey said. "I offer it to all the ladies who come to the church."

"What would the police find if they searched the vicarage and the church?" I asked. "Perhaps remnants of the poison you used on Cora. And what about the knife you used to stab Iris? I bear an injury from the blade. Were you the man I accosted in the salon a few evenings ago?"

"My dear lady, I don't know what you're talking about," Father Kersey said. "I'm sorry you were injured, but when you undertake dangerous tasks meant for men with years of training, you can't expect anything less."

"Quite right, Father. Miss Vale is a menace and a nuisance," Detective Chief Inspector Taylor said.

I clenched my hands. "Cora was on to you. And so was Iris. You had to silence them. You're a young fellow. What are you, thirty? It's possible you climbed up the drainpipe outside Cora's bedroom while she slept in the Rusty Nail," I said. "Or perhaps you slipped into the kitchen and placed the poison in the milk while Maudie checked on a noise at the front of the pub. Did you smash the flowerpot?"

"You should write fiction rather than florid obituary notices," Detective Chief Inspector Taylor said with a smirk. "Father Kersey, we shall keep you no longer. I suggest this evening draws to a close immediately."

"I shall decide that. This is *my* dinner party," Lady M said.

"I daresay none of us has an appetite after this unpleasant drama." Detective Chief Inspector Taylor glared at me. "I shall ruminate on how best to deal with you. Come along, Sergeants." He strode from the room.

Father Kersey followed swiftly, as did Lady Fairfax. Only Camille remained, still scribbling in her notepad, and Gil, whose expression flickered between surprise and indignation, as though he couldn't decide how to feel.

"Oh dear," Lady M said to me. "That didn't go as planned."

"I'd hoped Father Kersey would break down and confess," I replied with a frustrated sigh. "However, with Detective Chief Inspector Taylor standing by him, he found the backbone to resist."

"You're not giving up, are you?" Gil asked. "He's got guilt written all over his sweaty face. I never trusted the geezer. Iris said he gave her the creeps because he was so hands-on with the women, if you get my meaning." Gil mimed holding two large melons.

"Is that so? Would any of them be prepared to testify that he acted inappropriately?" I asked.

"Iris said he always kept things just legit enough, but she never felt easy around him. He was always talking about fallen women and redeeming them in a ceremony. Something odd went on when he got them behind closed doors."

"Perhaps he grabbed more melons," Lady M said.

"I suspect you're right. I'm not giving up," I said. "Father Kersey is the killer. I just need to make him confess. And I know exactly how to do it."

"I'm not sure this is a good idea," Sergeant Matthers muttered.

He stood beside me outside Saint Mary's church the following afternoon, shifting uncomfortably from foot to foot. Sergeant Redcote stood on my other side, equally ill at ease.

"This is where Father Kersey confesses his sins," I said. "After such a revealing evening, he must feel the urge to repent. He lied to all of us last night, so it'll weigh heavily on his conscience."

"If the man has a conscience," Sergeant Redcote muttered. "I've been looking into his past with Sergeant

Matthers. I had to make a few telephone calls, but the local police in Cardiff finally opened up."

I turned to him. "And?"

"Father Kersey had a terrible reputation. It's likely why he moved all the way to London to start afresh without his reputation following him."

"He continued to use brothels even after entering the priesthood?" I asked.

"There were rumours," Sergeant Redcote said, "but no one wanted to talk openly. Still, the rumours persisted. Parishioners left his church because they were unhappy."

"His diocese must have moved him," I said. "It's not unheard of. If a priest proves difficult or ill-suited to a parish, he's relocated. Sweep the problem onto someone else's rug."

"I feel uncomfortable about what you're asking us to do," Sergeant Matthers said. "And I doubt Saint Mary's priest will agree to it."

"My contact is distracting the priest," I assured him. "He'll be none the wiser. But I need you here as reliable witnesses. If I get a confession out of Father Kersey, Detective Chief Inspector Taylor won't believe me."

"Sometimes he doesn't even believe us," Sergeant Redcote said.

"He'll have to believe it when there are two of you."

Sergeant Matthers nodded. "We'll make him see sense."

"I had Gil watching Father Kersey last night," I said. "He was up late, so he was up to something, but he didn't leave the vicarage. There could still be evidence at his home or at the church. If we can find where he hid

Iris's body, that will be evidence even Detective Chief Inspector Taylor can't ignore."

"Here he comes!" Sergeant Redcote stiffened, his gaze on the end of the busy London street.

"Hurry. Inside, both of you," I said. "Sergeant Redcote, hide around the back of the confessional. It'll be a squeeze, but I'll go in with Sergeant Matthers. You'll need to do the talking, Sergeant, since Father Kersey will never believe a female priest."

"I'll do my best to sound as if I know what I'm doing." Sergeant Matthers dashed along with me, and we took up position, closing the door behind us and squeezing onto the small, hard wooden seat in the confessional box.

I had no concerns that the church's priest would interfere, since Gil was currently deep in conversation with him about joining the priesthood. At least, that was what I'd told him to do. However, Gil was my wild card, so anything could be going on.

I breathed in deeply and paused. That smell! I'd noticed it several times during the investigation but hadn't been able to place it. It showed how often I frequented a church not to recognise the pungent tang of incense. It was only natural that such a smell would cling to a priest's clothing.

Rapid footsteps approached the confessional box. The door opened and was swiftly shut. There was shuffling on the other side, and then the words I had been waiting to hear.

"Forgive me, Father, for I have sinned." It was Father Kersey.

Sergeant Matthers slowly slid back the dividing door between the confessionals, revealing the grill. He gently cleared his throat. "How long has it been since your last confession?"

"Three days. And I am full of sin. It is drowning me." Father Kersey's voice was hoarse.

"I understand. There is something you wish to reveal? The trials you have been going through?" Sergeant Matthers glanced at me. Wedged so close, I could smell the peppermint on his breath. I gave him a firm nod to continue.

"There is."

"Please go on."

There was silence for a few seconds. "Are you unwell? Your voice sounds different."

"I'm recovering from a cold, but I'm quite well. Please continue."

There was more shuffling. "I have lied to so many people. But... I had to do it. I must remain free to continue my work with the parish's fallen women. There are so many of them needing my help. My ceremonies return them to a pure, chaste state."

"You do good work. But you know, lying is a sin," Sergeant Matthers intoned in a suitably serious tone, while pinching his nose to make it sound like he was bunged up.

"Which is why I'm here!" Father Kersey said. "But I must do whatever it takes to ensure my good work continues."

"We all follow a higher purpose," Sergeant Matthers said gently. "Cleanse yourself of your lies, and then you can go about your excellent work. Your deceit will be forgiven."

There was a soft sigh. "My name has been associated with two murders. I know killing is wrong, but surely God understands when those deaths stop good people from being betrayed."

I clamped a hand over my mouth to stop from gasping. Was that a confession?

"God doesn't look kindly on those who take another's life," Sergeant Matthers said.

"But I had to do it. Those wicked women would have stopped me. They were threatening to ruin my good name." Father Kersey was almost panting from the tension. "I've done so much for this parish. Helped so many women, but there are still more who need my support, my love, and my encouragement."

"You took two lives to save many more?" Sergeant Matthers asked.

"Yes! God knows I follow his guidance. Cora and Iris were beyond helping. They lied and told me they'd found a righteous path to travel, when all they'd discovered was a new way to exploit vulnerable men. Naïve men, who knew no better. They tempted them with their lascivious ways and their silken words. It turned my stomach when I learned the truth. And when I visited Cora, and she laughed when I told her what would happen when she met our Saviour..." Father Kersey sucked in a shallow breath. "I had to do something. She said I was impure, the naïve one, and she'd show everybody my wicked lies and falsehoods."

"So, you acted in the name of God?" Sergeant Matthers asked. "You committed this sin to stop a woman who was beyond redemption?"

"Yes! And when I silenced her, goodness poured over me. It was the sign I'd been waiting for, and I knew I'd done the right thing. I am right, aren't I?"

"What about the other woman? Iris?" Sergeant Matthers asked.

"She was just as crooked. Iris kept a copy of the lies written about me. And I discovered she conducted the same wicked services as Cora. She promised me when she left Cora's house of sin that she'd seen the light. All she'd discovered was a way to make more money. I begged her to change her wicked ways, but she was just like Cora. I knew then I was vulnerable if she remained alive."

Sergeant Matthers looked at me again. We had a confession, but concrete proof of the murders was essential.

"The body," I mouthed silently to him.

"Before I can absolve you of your sins, do you know anything about Iris's body?" Sergeant Matthers asked.

"How... how do you know about that?" Father Kersey replied.

"God speaks to all of us," Sergeant Matthers said after a second of baffled silence. "Iris was beyond saving, but she still deserves a burial."

"You're a good man for thinking of her afterlife, but I will see to that," Father Kersey said. "There is a funeral tomorrow at my church. Iris is already in the ground, covered over. The coffin will go on top of her. I'm conducting the service, so I will say words for Iris. I won't name her directly, but she'll find peace. Although I can't guarantee what that will be. God will make that decision."

That was all we needed. When we found Iris's body, Father Kersey's freedom would be gone forever.

I slipped out of the confessional box and yanked open his door. He blinked and gasped when he saw me. "Miss Vale!"

"Father Kersey. I believe that was the most deranged confession I've ever heard," I said. "God won't help you out of this pickle."

Sergeant Matthers and Sergeant Redcote emerged, and Father Kersey shrank back, his eyes wide and mouth hanging open in shock.

"You'd better come with us, Father," Sergeant Matthers said. "You have some explaining to do."

I lounged on Ruby's chaise longue with Benji, waiting for her to return from the bathroom. I'd dashed over bright and early the next morning to update her on our spectacular arrest.

True to Father Kersey's confession, when the police examined an open grave waiting to be filled, they discovered Iris wrapped in the rug she'd fallen on, hidden beneath a thin layer of dirt.

After that damning evidence, Detective Chief Inspector Taylor had no choice but to search the vicarage and church and interview the women who received Father Kersey's so-called services. Let's just say it was a practical ceremony, remembered for all the wrong reasons.

And the help Father Kersey needed to move Iris? He'd recruited poor Mary and Julie and demanded they move the rug without telling them what was inside! Those women needed another bottle of gin and a slab of chocolate to get over the shock.

The police had also discovered the poison used to kill Cora hidden behind a pile of old paint tins in the vicarage shed and a notepad Father Kersey must have taken from Cora's room in the Rusty Nail, thinking it was her journal. The paper matched the scrap I'd found in her waste bin.

"We can't get too used to this luxury," I said to Benji.

He wagged his tail, seemingly most content with our current situation.

"Whatever is keeping that girl?" Lady M returned from a short stroll around the garden.

"How is Ruby feeling?" I asked.

"Tired. And still complaining of back pain, but she has a better appetite," Lady M said. "I must show you the nursery. I had everything delivered last week. It's beautifully fitted out."

"I imagine it's delightful," I said. "I'm at a loss what to buy Ruby as a gift when the happy day arrives. I have no experience with infants and their needs. Puppies and kittens I can manage, but this is a new adventure for all of us."

"Indeed, it is, but one I'm looking forward to," Lady M said. "I was becoming worried I would grow old and wither away, alone on this vast estate. But now, with

Ruby and the baby settled here, it'll be good to have new life and all the excitement and energy it brings."

"I'm happy it's worked out so well," I said.

"Make sure you're not a stranger," Lady M said. "Babies are noisy and make the most extraordinary smells, but we shall need your support."

"I'm going nowhere," I replied. "Perhaps I'll invest in earmuffs, though. I find babies' shrieks grate on the nerves."

"What a splendid idea! Perhaps you could treat me to some, too."

There was a thump on the stairs and a small cry for help. I sprang to my feet with Benji at my heels. When we got to the grand entranceway, Ruby clung to the banister, her face slick with sweat.

I dashed up to join her. "Did you fall?"

"It's much more terrifying than that." Ruby gasped for breath. "I think the baby is on its way!"

Historical Notes

Here are a couple of information nuggets you might find of interest.

Soho in 1920s London

By the 1920s, Soho had already earned its reputation as London's immoral playground. It was a patchwork of narrow streets filled with coffee houses, boarding rooms, music halls, and places that were polite by day and scandalous by night.

Prostitution wasn't new here. For centuries, London'ssporting ladies and public women had been working in and around the West End.But the Great War changed the trade. Thousands of young men on leave had fuelled demand, while wartime dislocation and losing male breadwinners pushed many women into sex work to survive. By 1920, the war was over, but the economic hardship wasn't. And neither was the demand.

Soho became a hub because it was cosmopolitan, anonymous, and easy to reach. The area's mix of immigrants, artists, waiters, musicians, and theatre folk made it less judgmental than other parts of London. The clientele ranged from dockers and cabbies to aristocrats.

Some women worked the streets—Rupert Street, Brewer Street, and Old Compton Street were well-known pitches—while others operated from "houses" above cafés or lodging rooms rented by the night.

The law was a murky business. Street solicitation was an offence under the *Solicitation for Immoral Purposes Act* (part of the 1912 Criminal Law Amendment Act), but proving it was tricky unless a woman was caught accosting passersby with her trade. Brothels were illegal under the *Disorderly Houses Act*, but many kept operating under the noses (and sometimes with the coin in the palm) of the police.

Pimps, known then as bullies or blokes, often hung about to protect their women from drunks and to take a cut of earnings. Some women worked independently, while others were part of more organised madams' houses, where drinks, dancing, and sex were all part of the evening.

When you picture it, think dimly lit streets, the smell of roasting coffee and cigarette smoke, gramophone music drifting from a club doorway, and women with bobbed hair and smart coats, scanning the crowd for customers under the flicker of a gas lamp.

The Rusty Nail

There are no London pubs with this name, but there is a cozy little place in Aberdeen called the Rusty Nail.

There is also an adorable place at the foot of the Urris Hills on the Wild Atlantic Way in Ireland. The pub has an open fire, a delicious-sounding menu, and it settled in my mind because at the time of writing this book (summer 2025) I was applying to become a dual citizen of Ireland and the UK.

Perhaps when I become an Irish citizen, I shall visit my ancestors' place of birth and raise a glass of Guinness to them at the Rusty Nail.

Also by

Death at the Fireside Inn
Death at the Drunken Duck
Death at the Craven Arms
Death at the Dripping Tap
Death at the Harbour Arms
Death at the Swan Tavern
Death at the Jolly Cricketer
Death at the Green Man
Death at the Rusty Nail
Death at the Thistle Inn
More mysteries coming soon. While you wait, why not investigate K.E. O'Connor's back catalogue (Kitty's alter ego.)

About the author

Immerse yourself into Kitty Kildare's cleverly woven historical British mysteries. Follow the mystery in the Veronica Vale Investigates series and enjoy the dazzle and delights of 1920s England.

Kitty is a not-so-secret pen name of established cozy mystery author K.E.O'Connor, who decided she wanted to time travel rather than cast spells! Enjoy the twists and turns.

Join in the fun and get Kitty's newsletter (and secret wartime files about our sleuthing ladies!)

Newsletter: https://BookHip.com/JJPKDLB
Website: www.kittykildare.com
Facebook: www.facebook.com/kittykildare

Printed in Dunstable, United Kingdom